MR. DARCY'S COURTESAN

A PRIDE AND PREJUDICE VARIATION

Valerie Lennox

Punk Rawk Books

MR. DARCY'S COURTESAN
© 2019 by Valerie Lennox
www.vjchambers.com

Punk Rawk Books

All characters appearing in this work are fictitious. Any resemblance to real persons, living or dead, is purely coincidental.

All rights reserved. No part of this book may be used or reproduced in any manner whatsoever without written permission except in the case of brief quotations embodied in critical articles and reviews

ISBN: 9781091353183

Printed in the United States of America

10 9 8 7 6 5 4 3 2 1

MR. DARCY'S COURTESAN

A PRIDE AND PREJUDICE VARIATION

Valerie Lennox

CHAPTER ONE

Lydia Bennet picked at the dress she was wearing, a blue morning dress that was a tad bit too big for her figure. She always resented wearing the clothes that Elizabeth and Jane asked her to wear in the house they shared with their younger sisters Kitty and Mary. She wanted to wear her own clothes, even though they would only raise questions from the younger girls about Lydia's position in the world. The clothes Elizabeth gave her to wear in their house were sedate and staid and proper, unlike the rest of Lydia's wardrobe, heaven knew.

Their mother had resided in their house until recently, when she'd taken ill suddenly. She'd only battled two weeks with the sickness before succumbing, leaving the girls orphans in the world. It had now been five years since their father had passed on.

Elizabeth eyed her younger sister, trying to gauge what was going on in Lydia's mind. She knew the answer was likely precious little, since Lydia was one of the more empty-headed people she had ever known. Still, the family had to be grateful for Lydia, who gave them some financial support, even if the younger girls were unaware. And Elizabeth knew that Lydia didn't have to do it, nor did she have to conceal her identity for the well-being of the Bennet name. She did that because she had a heart, even if she had no head.

"I thought," said Jane in a quiet voice, "that you had some arrangement with Mr. Chivsworth."

"Oh, no," said Lydia, sighing. "It turns out Mr.

Chivsworth is only interested in virgins, and heaven knows, I am not for him."

"Lydia, don't use such language!" Jane recoiled, peering into her tea cup. There wasn't much tea these days, and there certainly wasn't anything to serve with it besides bread and butter. Usually day-old bread at that, which was all that could be gotten.

There had been times in the family's history when they had been better of financially, but after their mother's death, they had discovered she had left behind gambling debts, and they were so severe that even Lydia could not pay them off. Not that Jane would have allowed them to take such a sum from Lydia, at any rate. The amount of profit from Lydia's lifestyle that the eldest Miss Bennet could tolerate was only the bare minimum. It was day-old bread, then, and skimping and scraping where they could.

"What?" scoffed Lydia. "Virgin? Lord, Jane, that's a word from the *bible*."

"What if one of the younger girls overhears?" said Jane.

"They won't," said Lydia. "You forbid them near the room when we are discussing finances." For all the younger girls knew, Lydia worked outside of the home as a governess, and she contributed to the household that way. She only came home once a month, on a Tuesday, and after greeting her younger sisters, they were shooed off while the others talked about money. Both of the younger Miss Bennets resented this, as Lydia was the youngest of them all, but in the time that had passed since the death of their father, all of the girls had lost a great deal of whatever sparks that fed them before.

"So, then are you engaged with anyone now?" said Elizabeth, setting down her tea cup. It was easier if Lydia had a regular patron. She had been in a longterm arrangement once with the duke of Somerset, and she had been quite comfortable—indeed they all had—for the year that it had lasted. The duke gave her use of his carriage, and gave her a monthly stipend, and escorted her to balls and parties and dinners. But then they had quarreled and parted ways.

Elizabeth had been furious with Lydia. How could the girl have quarreled with a duke? Lydia had sniffed and said that the duke liked her *because* she was a spitfire. She had simply pushed a bit too far. She had not expected him to break it all off.

"Well, no," said Lydia. "Not on a regular basis, but I am accompanying Mr. Southson to a ball on Saturday and if we get on well, perhaps we will form a more permanent arrangement."

Jane's face looked pinched. "So, in other words, you have no income at all at the moment?"

Lydia shrugged. "You make it sound so dire, Jane, honestly."

"Well," said Jane, "it's not good, and you must realize that."

"You mean Mama's debts," said Lydia.

"Yes," said Jane. "She had gambling debts so large that we are all in danger of being carted off to debtor's prison. I don't understand why I need to keep repeating this to you. Things *are* dire."

Lydia set down her tea cup. "I don't know what it is that you want me to do. I can't force men into a relationship with me. I'm not a common whore. I don't charge by the night."

"Well, I don't know," said Jane, "perhaps you might flirt a bit more or something. You were always very good at flirting."

"I am doing my best," said Lydia, drawing herself up. "Honestly, I hate being here. Everyone is so depressed in this house." She turned away.

"We are in mourning," snapped Jane, getting to her feet.

"Half mourning," countered Lydia. "And I don't see why it matters, since none of you are ever out in society anyway. And that's not my fault, it's Lizzy's."

"That's not my fault, it's Lady Catherine's," Elizabeth countered coolly.

"Oh, not this again," said Jane. "I'm going to check on the other girls." She swept out of the room.

Elizabeth sighed and reached for the last piece of bread and butter. "Now, you've upset Jane again."

"She's always upset." Lydia slumped. "Oh, Lizzy, I can't bear her. Ever since Mama died, she has been in utter despair at every waking moment. I know she is an old maid with no prospects, but you are practically as old as she is, and you manage to be cheery."

"Do I?" Elizabeth raised her eyebrows.

"Certainly," said Lydia. "When we are planning out my dresses or when we are planning my balls, you are quite in good spirits."

Elizabeth grimaced. "Don't say that."

"Oh, I suppose you should be as dreary as she is," said Lydia. "You know what she should do, is *she* should be a companion to Mr. Chivsworth herself. She was always the beauty of the family, and she is still lovely, even at her age. And then maybe she wouldn't be in such an awful mood."

Elizabeth's lips parted in shock.

"Oh, Lord, I'm *jesting.*" Lydia shook her head. She stood up. "Listen, perhaps I shall take my leave. You can tell Jane that I send her my love."

"Lydia, wait," said Elizabeth.

Lydia turned to her. "Yes?"

"This Chivsworth, you say he is really only interested in virgins?"

"Yes," said Lydia. "He wants a woman unspoiled, who has no knowledge of carnal pleasures. But maddeningly, he is not interested in a woman who knows nothing of the world. He wants a woman with some experience in society, someone he can also converse with. I told him there is no such woman." She cocked her head. "Although, to be truthful, Jane would be perfect for him."

8

"And the sum of money he would settle on this virginal woman?" said Elizabeth. "Did you not say it was more than enough to pay off Mama's debts?"

"Listen, what are you about? You know Jane would never—"

"It was a lot of money, was it not?" Elizabeth's voice was quiet but fierce.

"Yes, it was," said Lydia. She sat back down. "Why are you pursuing this?"

"Perhaps I could do it," said Elizabeth, swallowing hard.

"What?" said Lydia.

"Quiet," said Elizabeth. "Jane might hear you."

* * *

Years ago, in the aftermath of their father's death, Lydia had managed to become someone's mistress. No one of any importance—a colonel in the militia, actually. He happened to also be the third son of a viscount, however, with the sort of connections that Lydia could exploit.

Not that she would have, of course, not without Elizabeth's help.

Elizabeth never would have encouraged any of it, not if life had been as it was before the incident at Rosings, the one that changed the course for her and all her family. Elizabeth knew that she had been set up by Lady Catherine, and she learned later it was because Lady Catherine knew that Mr. Darcy had proposed to Elizabeth, and Lady Catherine was not going to let anyone marry her nephew except her own daughter.

What Lady Catherine didn't seem to understand was that Elizabeth had refused that proud man, and she had no interest in marrying him.

Well, perhaps after that letter, in which Darcy had explained a great many things about Mr. Wickham and about how he had interpreted Jane's shyness as indifference, perhaps she wondered...

But it didn't matter. It had all gone as Lady Catherine

wanted. As far as Elizabeth knew, Mr. Darcy was quite happy with his wife, the former Miss de Bourgh.

And with the Bennet reputation already in tatters, none of it mattered. She had brought shame on all of them, and she regretted that. But nothing in her could have ever induced to her to marry that wretched, wretched Cumberbottom. No, Darcy would have been a prince compared to that man. She would have even preferred Mr. Collins to Cumberbottom, and that was saying something.

Maybe if things had been different, her father could have arranged something else for her, and that might have saved the family, but then her father was in that awful carriage accident, and he was killed, and, well, Lydia exploiting the connections of a viscount seemed the best they could all do.

As Mr. Darcy had pointed out all those years ago, the Bennets did not have impressive connections, so no one in the higher echelons of the ton had any idea who Lydia was. She went by the last name of Swan, and she was one of the most sought-after courtesans in London. Partly this was because of Lydia's own vivacity and temperament. She was fearless, and she was willing to try anything. But it was also because of Elizabeth's guidance.

Elizabeth had steered the ship from the beginning, and Lydia had welcomed her help and also vowed to use whatever money she had to help the rest of the family.

So, together, they had determined what had to be done. They had studied the fashions and made sure that Lydia was attired properly. They had rented a box at the opera so that Lydia could be seen and desired by all. They had made sure that Lydia had a house in the fashionable part of town. None of these things were cheap, but they were investments, and they were worth it. Lydia commanded quite a bit of money.

She could not keep it all, of course. The upkeep of Lydia's lifestyle was expensive. And she gave as much as she could convince Jane to take to the family.

Of course, the discovery of Mrs. Bennet's gambling debts

had been quite a blow. None of them had realized how bad it was at the time, and now there was nothing to be done about it except to pay them off. Which they couldn't do, not even with Lydia's help.

Once upon a time, Elizabeth would never have considered being involved in such a thing as the commerce of her sister's body. She would have been appalled by it all. But so many things had changed since then, and Elizabeth had become practical.

Lydia's lifestyle, in all truth, was not that much different than any other woman's. When she was in a relationship with a man, he saw to all of her needs financially, as if he were her husband. The only difference was that Lydia didn't have to stay with that man forever and that she got to keep her money when he was gone. There were advantages to it all. Certainly, Lydia was never going to be allowed entrance at the best dinners and parties, but then neither was Elizabeth. The places Lydia *was* invited, however, were often regal and marvelous.

However, it was possible Elizabeth was only telling herself these things because she had essentially agreed to become a courtesan herself.

But as she was trying to explain to Lydia in her sister's house across London, it was not going to be that way. "It will only be this once, with this Chivsworth, and then I will never do it again. We will tell the others I've gotten a position as a governess—"

"Oh, so we're both governesses?" broke in Lydia.

"Well, what else can I say?" said Elizabeth.

"Perhaps that you will be chaperoning some daughter of someone or other," said Lydia.

"That's much the same thing," said Elizabeth. "Whatever the case, it will be temporary. I will only be part of the arrangement until the man tires of me, which I rather imagine will be soon if he only desires virgins. Because once he has despoiled me, then I shall no longer intrigue him."

Elizabeth took a long breath.

Elizabeth knew that it was also improper for her to be out and about in society while she was mourning her mother's death, but of the two sins, she thought that selling her body was so much more dire that it canceled the other out.

Lydia bit down on her bottom lip. "Listen, Lizzy—"

The door to the sitting room burst open and George Wickham appeared in the doorway.

"Georgie!" said Lydia, putting both her hands on her hips. "Didn't I tell you not to sneak past the butler anymore?"

Wickham spread his hands. "Do I hear this right? Miss Elizabeth getting despoiled?"

Elizabeth drew herself up. "Would you get rid of him, Lydia?"

"You are to be announced," said Lydia to Wickham. "You're not to be traipsing around the house on your own, stealing things."

Wickham clutched his chest. "Oh, I'm wounded. Steal from you, Lyddie? I would never."

"You have," said Lydia. "More than once."

Elizabeth could not begin to comprehend the relationship between Lydia and Wickham. For some reason, Lydia tolerated the man, even though he was horrible. His fortune had not improved since he'd been dismissed from the militia and now he drifted through London from scheme to scheme, sometimes on top with some gambling winnings, but usually begging for funds from anyone he knew of, even Lydia.

She thought that Lydia might have still found Wickham charming, in some sad way. Or maybe Lydia simply felt sorry for him. Elizabeth wasn't sure.

"No," said Wickham. "I would never do such an awful thing to such a beautiful lady." He threw himself down on a chair opposite Elizabeth and grinned. "Now, tell me about

being despoiled again?"
"I refuse to speak to you," said Elizabeth.
"The high and mighty Miss Elizabeth," said Wickham. "Too good for the likes of me, even though her name has been dragged through the dirt by all of good society."
"What my sister chooses to do with Mr. Chivsworth is her own business," said Lydia.
"Lydia!" Elizabeth protested. "You are giving things away to him."
"Oh, sorry," said Lydia, wrinkling up her nose.
Yes, not a brain in her head. Elizabeth sighed.
"Mr. Chivsworth, is it?" said Wickham. He leered at her. "Lucky man."
Elizabeth felt strongly as though she might vomit.
Lydia went over to Wickham, grabbed him by the hand, and hauled him up out of the seat. "Out. Go to the front door, like I've told you, Georgie."
He winked at her. "I'm not here asking for anything, Lyddie."
Lydia sighed and crossed the room to find her reticule. She took out a few coins and pressed them into Wickham's hand. "There. Now, off with you."
"You don't need to do that," said Wickham, who was already shoving the money into his pocket. "I can't accept anything."
"Go," said Lydia, pointing at the door.
He kissed her on the cheek. "You're a dove."
"*Goodbye*, Georgie."
Chuckling, he left.
Lydia shut the door after him. "Oh, thank the Lord."
"I don't see why you put up with him," said Elizabeth. "Or why you give him money."
"With Wickham, it's better to pay up if you want rid of him," said Lydia.
"It's more than that." Elizabeth arched her eyebrows. "You care about him."

"Don't be ridiculous!" Lydia laughed airily. "For Georgie?"

"You call him by a nickname. He calls you—"

"I don't care for him at all," said Lydia. She crossed the room. "Let's stop talking about him. If you are really serious about this Chivsworth business, then we have a lot of preparation to do."

"Of course I'm serious, and you mustn't try to talk me out of it. I need to do this for the family."

"You realize, Lizzy, if you were to meet a man later—"

"I won't."

"But you'll never be able to get married—"

"We are a houseful of spinsters, and you know it." Elizabeth squared her shoulders. "There is nothing to risk on that score. The only thing I fear is the knowledge of who I am getting out. There is a bit of infamy attached to me after what happened at Rosings. No one speaks of it anymore, but if anyone were to remember who I was, to put it all together—"

"We will transform you," said Lydia. "No one will even recognize you."

"Good," said Elizabeth. "Then let's get started."

CHAPTER TWO

Fitzwilliam Darcy would rather not be in London. It wasn't that he hated London, not exactly. In fact, at one point in time in his life, he would have said that he liked the society of friends and the pace of it all. While he did not like being crowded into spaces with strangers, he was not averse to the warm friendship of those he already knew, and he rather liked witty conversation.

But he liked little these days.

For as long as he could manage, he had stayed in mourning for his late wife, but the time for that being acceptable had passed. Society was less forgiving of a bachelor who remained in mourning for a long period of time, anyway. The thought was that he needed to get back out there and find another wife.

After all, he had come out of this marriage with no heir.

But that very thought caused him to crumble inside. He got up from his desk and crossed the room to find a bottle of whiskey. He was about to pour himself a drink when there was a knock at the door.

He set down the bottle. "Yes?"

A footman appeared in the doorway. "Sir? It's a Mr. Wickham in the sitting room downstairs."

"Wickham?" Darcy's jaw tightened. "You let him in?"

"Was I not supposed to?" said the footman, looking a bit worried.

Darcy sighed heavily. "Oh, dash it all. Now that he's inside, you'd have to haul him out bodily, and then he'd probably stand outside on the street and make a scene." And that might upset Georgiana. "I'll be down in a moment."

The first time that Mr. Wickham had darkened Mr. Darcy's door after the incident with Georgiana, Darcy had thrown him into the street himself, with his own hands. And Wickham was lucky that Darcy hadn't knocked him down with his fists as well.

The second time that Wickham arrived, Darcy had just gotten married, and he was feeling charitable, and he'd let the blackguard in, but he hadn't given in when Wickham asked for money.

The third time...

Well, the point was that Wickham had worn him down. Darcy wasn't sure what kind of man had so little pride that he would keep coming begging from a man who he had wronged and who despised him, but apparently Wickham was that kind of man. It was easiest to give him a little something. Never much, of course, but enough to see him through, and then there would be no more Wickham for months.

That is, if Wickham managed to gain entry. Darcy had told the staff at Pemberley to bar the door to him, and they did. The staff at his London house changed over more regularly, though, and they weren't always as good at getting rid of him. Wickham was more likely to appear in London, also, which was unfortunate.

Darcy poured himself a few fingers' worth of the whiskey and downed it in a gulp. He felt the liquid coursing a warm path into his stomach, but he didn't know if it had done much to lessen his annoyance at seeing Wickham.

No matter. He had said he would see him. That was all there was to it.

He hurried to the sitting room and opened the door.

When he entered, Wickham stood up, not that Darcy cared how polite the man was pretending to be while he begged for money he didn't deserve.

"Darcy!" said Wickham, smiling broadly.

"What do you want?" said Darcy, striding across the room without meeting Wickham's eye.

"Now, who says I want anything?" Wickham sat back down in his chair, getting comfortable. "Perhaps I've just come to see my old boyhood chum."

"Have you?" said Darcy, eyeing him.

"How have you been?" said Wickham.

"In mourning," Darcy said flatly.

"Oh, right, yes," said Wickham. "So sorry about Mrs. Darcy. Terrible shame. And the babe too, I hear. At least it was only a girl."

Darcy rounded on him. "Out."

"Pardon me?"

Darcy pointed at the door. "I don't have to listen to this, to you. Get out of my house now."

"Oh, Lord, Darcy, you're in a bad mood." Wickham chortled. He didn't move.

Darcy marched back to the other side of the room and opened the door. "Get. Out. Now."

"You know," said Wickham, not budging from his chair, "I just saw Miss Elizabeth Bennet today. That was what reminded me of you in the first place. I saw her, and I remembered that she *hated* you, and I thought, 'I should stop by and see old Darcy again, shouldn't I?'"

Darcy paused at the door. Elizabeth Bennet. Now that was a name he hadn't heard in a while. He'd always felt a little grim about what had become of her. More than once, he'd thought of trying to call on her and offer for her again. Or to offer something to help her.

It had been his fault she'd been caught up in that business. He knew his aunt must have been responsible for it all. But then Mr. Bennet had been killed suddenly, and the whole family had been turned out of the household by Mr. Collins, who inherited Longbourn. The speed of that was likely due to his aunt's influence on Collins as well, he thought. But, at any rate, he'd lost track of her. "You see Miss Elizabeth? She allows you to call on her?"

"Well, not exactly," said Wickham. "She's not nearly as nice to me as she used to be. Probably your fault, I wager. You're always turning people against me." Wickham fussed with his cravat as if this was always being turned against him by Darcy as well.

"So, then, how did you see her? Where is she? Is she in London?"

Wickham grinned. "Oh, so it's like that, is it?" He sat up straighter. "I heard rumors that you proposed to her and that she turned you down flat, but I thought it had to be rot. Because someone like you would never lower himself so far as to offer for the likes of her. But maybe there was some truth to it."

Darcy shook his head. There was no point in continuing this conversation. It wasn't worth any knowledge that Wickham might give him. Besides which, he didn't care about Miss Elizabeth. Why should he, after all? "Never mind it, Wickham. I need you to go."

"I know all manner of wicked things about Miss Elizabeth," said Wickham. "And I could tell you an earful. But it'll cost you."

"Lord, Wickham, don't be ridiculous," said Darcy. "I'm not paying you for gossip."

"She's right on the brink of becoming notorious, if I understand it myself." Wickham made a tent with his fingers and rested them under his chin.

"Notorious? What are you talking about?"

"As I say, it'll cost you."

Darcy rolled his eyes, but he found himself shutting the door. "Fine. How much money do you want this time?"

Wickham named an amount.

"Have you lost your mind?" said Darcy. "No." He started to open the door again.

Wickham named another, significantly lower amount.

"She is in London. I know her address."

Darcy made a disgusted face. But he stalked across the room, taking a key out of his breast pocket as he did so. He used the key to unlock a drawer in one of his desks and he found some money there. He counted out what Wickham had asked for and showed it to the man.

Wickham got up, hand out.

"No," said Darcy. "Tell me first, and then you'll get your money."

"The way I understand it," said Wickham. "She's going to become Mr. Chivsworth's mistress."

"Mistress?" said Darcy. "But she is—" He broke off. Well, she was not of such an elevated station, actually, and it was his fault. "I still don't think she would ever do such a thing."

"I think the family is in financial distress," said Wickham. "They're dealing with gambling debts left behind by their late mother."

Oh, so Mrs. Bennet was gone as well? Darcy had never liked the woman, but he was sorry for it. He knew what it was like to have lost both parents, and it was difficult. "Chivsworth?" Darcy shook his head. "I've never met him." But he had heard of the man. He was a baronet, so Darcy thought.

"Really? I've met Chivsworth," said Wickham.

"Oh, well, capital," said Darcy sarcastically.

" Chivsworth never has a mistress, because he only wants to bed virgins."

Darcy's lip curled. "That is positively—"

" Willing to pay lots of money for it, I imagine," said Wickham.

"How would Miss Bennet even be privy to such things?" said Darcy. "She would have no connection to someone like Chivsworth."

"Her sister, most likely."

"Which sister?"

"Oh, right," said Wickham. "I'd forgotten that you don't

know that either. You've heard of Miss Lydia Swan, I assume?"

"The courtesan?" said Darcy. "Why, yes, I even saw her from afar at one of those balls at Cartwright's. Colonel Fitzwilliam is always dragging me to them. She was…" He trailed off, and then he realized that she had looked a little familiar. "Lydia Swan is actually Lydia Bennet."

"That's right," said Wickham. "She really is the most fun of the Bennet sisters, I must say."

"Well if there is one woman of pleasure in the family, then why add to the number?" said Darcy. "Why can't Miss Lydia take up with Chivsworth?"

"Because he only wants virgins. I've explained this," said Wickham.

"And this is all because of gambling debts?"

"I believe so."

"You said you knew where Miss Elizabeth lived, did you not?"

* * *

Darcy didn't know why he found himself calling on the Bennet household the following morning. He had only the vaguest outline of a plan, and he wasn't entirely sure what it might comprise, but he'd been agitated since he'd received the news from Wickham.

He hadn't slept well, in fact. He didn't like thinking of the business. It was sordid.

Certainly, he no longer had feelings for Miss Elizabeth. He hadn't had feelings for her in quite some time, and even when he had, they'd been some kind of passing madness. He was not the sort of man who entered into an alliance with a woman like her, and he knew it. Even before his aunt had meddled and destroyed her reputation, she had been below him.

He had been taken with her bright eyes and her quick wit. The fact that she had not fawned all over him had been appealing as well. Most women seemed to fall all over themselves around him. They all wanted to secure their places as his wife, and not because of anything other than his station and his fortune. Elizabeth had seemed immune to that, and he had been charmed by it.

But she had not been interested, and even though he wondered if she might have changed her mind after that awful business with Cumberbottom, he was glad he'd never pursued it, because it would have been tainted, then. If she was only taking him because she had no other options, it wouldn't have meant the same thing.

And back then, he was young, and he was proud, and he was worried about how he might be perceived if he took a wife with a colorful past.

Now, none of that mattered. He didn't care much about anything anymore. He had felt gray and empty since Anne and the baby had died, and he hated himself for all of it. Anne had always been sickly. He should never have gotten her with child at all. And once she was with child, he'd taken her to the country, and he shouldn't have done that. And he'd allowed her to work with midwives, and not the accoucheurs that everyone raved about in London. He had as good as killed her.

He was no good to anyone, that was how Darcy saw it. He couldn't even get his sister married off, even though she'd been out in society for three seasons. Thinking he could help Elizabeth Bennet? It was folly. Thinking she'd want help from him? Ha. She'd just as likely spit in his face.

But here he was, heading to her home, and he had no idea what he was going to say to her.

What he did know was that ever since he had heard she was about to become Chivsworth's mistress, he'd had the most abominable visions of Elizabeth without her clothes in bed with that man, and he could not chase them from his mind. They were driving him to the brink of madness. He had never really even contemplated Elizabeth without her clothes before.

Well.

That was perhaps a lie, but he had not contemplated it for such a stretch of time, at any rate. He had stricken such an improper thought from his head at once, as was only right. At least, mostly, he had stricken them. Almost always.

It was going to be unbearable when she received him in her home and he looked at her, and he recalled that he had been imagining her bare skin.

He shouldn't go at all, in fact. He should turn around and go home.

Yes, that's exactly what he would do. He would turn around, and he would not visit the Bennet sisters. To do so would be quite insupportable.

CHAPTER THREE

Elizabeth did not know what to do with herself. What was Mr. Darcy doing here? How had Mr. Darcy even found them? Why would he call on them?

It was mortifying, because they had nothing to offer him, not even bread and butter, since they had kept all of that back for Lydia's visit the day before. There was nothing but tea and a bit of milk, and they were obliged to serve it to themselves, because they only paid for a maid of all work a few days of the week. The rest of the time she served another family in similar straits to themselves.

Elizabeth wished he would leave.

Mr. Darcy himself looked very uncomfortable. He kept coughing and saying the same stupid thing over and over. "It certainly has been a long time." The rest of the time, he was maddeningly silent.

Elizabeth remembered that he was rather bad at making conversation. She sipped at her tea. "Well, I daresay you're a busy man, Mr. Darcy."

"Busy?" said Darcy. "Well, not entirely, no."

"But certainly you have other things you need to attend to today. We would hate to keep you from them," said Elizabeth.

"Lizzy," admonished Jane. She smiled at Mr. Darcy. "You must forgive my sister. We are unaccustomed to having visitors. She has quite forgotten her manners."

"Oh, no, indeed," said Mr. Darcy. "I, um, that is, I…" He coughed. "It certainly has been a long time."

Elizabeth glared at him.

"Do you see Mr. Bingley much these days?" said Jane. "And his sisters?"

"Sometimes," said Darcy.

"And how are they?" said Jane.

"Oh, well," said Darcy. "Quite well."

"You must convey to them our greetings and well wishes, of course," said Jane.

"Indeed," said Darcy. He coughed. "Listen, I wonder if I might speak to Miss Elizabeth. Alone."

Elizabeth was so shocked, she stood up. There was really only one reason that a man asked to speak to a woman alone, and that was to propose, but... well, that could not be why Mr. Darcy was here.

"Oh," said Jane in a strange voice. "Why, of course. We will be happy to give you some privacy." She stood up. "Come Kitty. Mary."

Kitty stood up.

Elizabeth sat down. Mr. Darcy could not be proposing to her. He could not.

Mary sniffed.

"Mary," said Jane.

Mary eyed Mr. Darcy. "It was good to see you, sir."

Well, it was true that Mr. Darcy had proposed to Elizabeth before.

"And you as well," said Mr. Darcy.

But, no, Mr. Darcy was married already. He had married Anne de Bourgh, and so he could not be proposing. So, then why—

And then, suddenly, everyone had left the room, and it was only her and him.

She gulped at her tea. Her heart had started to race, and she couldn't understand why for the life of her.

Darcy coughed.

She squared her shoulders and waited. Her heart sped up. She drank more tea and set down her cup in her saucer with a clatter. " Well, Mr. Darcy, when a man asks to be alone with a woman, he usually has something to say. You had better come out with it." There, good. She didn't sound at all out of sorts. She even sounded a bit cold. Perfect.

"Yes," he said. "I suppose I must."

"Well?"

"I have heard something dreadful about you."

" Well, that is interesting, I suppose. " Her stomach turned over. "I had not thought anyone bothered to gossip about me anymore. I thought they had moved on to more recent scandals."

"No, don't worry. The person who told me doesn't seem likely to repeat it. He forced me to pay him for the information."

Her heart sank. "Mr. Wickham? You have been speaking to Mr. Wickham?"

Darcy swallowed, not meeting her gaze.

Oh, Lord, he knew everything. Wickham knew about Chivsworth. He had told Mr. Darcy.

Darcy stood up, looking agitated. "Listen, I don't want you to do it."

She stood up too. This was horrid. She was mortified. That Wickham had heard her plans to debase herself and had repeated them to Mr. Darcy, it was more than she could bear.

Mr. Darcy continued, "I know it is not my concern, but if the problem is simply that you need funds to cover your mother's debts, I would be happy to provide the necessary—"

"What?" She was shaking. She was angry and confused, and she didn't know what to think or to do. " How dare you?"

"I apologize," he said. "But you are the one who is about to surrender your virtue to some horrible man for compensation, so—"

"So, I don't deserve the decency of your keeping your

nose out of my affairs?" she demanded.

"Well, I must admit that I feel responsible for your situation. If my aunt had not gotten wind of my proposal, perhaps none of it would have happened in the first place."

"Perhaps not," said Elizabeth. "But I should not have been so stupid as to have allowed him to get me alone. I brought it on myself."

"I would like to help you."

"Just now? You've suddenly decided that you want to help? Where have you been for the past five years?"

"I lost track of you," he said. "No one knew where you went after your father's passing. And then, I was distracted, I suppose."

"With your marriage," she said.

"Yes."

"Congratulations, by the way," she said. "Belatedly."

He flinched. "I suppose you have not heard the news."

"What news?"

"My wife passed away."

"Oh." She looked at her feet. "I am sorry, sir. That is sad news indeed."

"Yes," he said.

They were quiet.

"Listen," he said. "I really do want to help."

"You'll hand over the money that we need, then, and be on your way? You'll want nothing in return?"

"Of course not."

"I don't need your charity, Mr. Darcy."

"Would you accept the money if I asked for something in return?"

"What would you ask for?"

He looked up at her, his gaze piercing.

She got the strange sensation that he could see through her clothing and she felt exposed and naked and frightened. A shiver went up her neck.

"If you're willing to do this for Chivsworth, then do it

for me instead."

She took a step backward, knocking over a chair.

His voice dropped in pitch. It was gravelly. " Be *my* mistress."

She gasped.

He shook himself and turned away. "Forgive me. I do not know why I said that."

Elizabeth did not know how she felt. She still felt exposed, possibly simply from the conversation that had occurred between them, possibly from that searing look he'd given her. He had never looked at her that way, not when they danced together, not when he proposed to her. Perhaps if he had…

But no, because it was a horrid way to look at her. It set her quite out of sorts, and she was not the least bit pleased about it. She should rebuke him for the look itself, let alone what he had just suggested. That, of course, was… was…

Oh, Elizabeth didn't know. Her heart had started beating fast again, and it was coursing blood through her body, making her feel warm and strange. The truth was, when she had thought of becoming Chivsworth's mistress, she'd not allowed herself any real time to consider the, er, physicality of the arrangement. She had assumed that she would get through that when it became necessary. To think on something like that would make her more likely to back out of the entire thing, and she needed to do this for her sisters.

But now, looking at Mr. Darcy, who wasn't even meeting her gaze anymore, whose head was downcast, whose shoulders were so frightfully broad, and who was in possession of a rather immensely deep voice, she found herself pondering possibilities. Thinking of what Mr. Darcy might look like if he were not wearing anything covering those shoulders, for instance.

Elizabeth did not ponder such things often. She knew what went on between men and women in bed now, though, even though she was not married. She could not have helped Lydia with her career if she had not had at least a rudimentary knowledge of how it all worked. She had to admit that it made her queasy to think on it very much, at least usually, but now that Mr. Darcy was—

She shook herself.

"I would ask that you leave, please, sir," she said, and her voice wasn't strong. It was the shadow of a voice, as if she were nothing but a shy girl. She hated that she sounded so weak.

"Yes, of course," said Mr. Darcy, lifting his gaze to hers. "But you must consider taking charity, I think, Miss Bennet. You cannot allow this awful thing to befall you. I cannot allow it. Why I will seek out your mother's debtors and—"

"You will do no such thing." Still the wavery voice, dash it all. "Please, go back to your life and forget about me again, please."

"I never forgot about you, Miss Bennet," he said quietly.

"Well, I forgot about you," she said, and now her voice was fierce, when she was lying.

He blinked and then nodded. "I do apologize again. I really should not have said— I don't know what came over me. That is, I am utterly—"

"Goodbye, Mr. Darcy."

"Goodbye," he said, and then he did leave.

Elizabeth sank down in a chair and tried to steady her beating heart.

CHAPTER FOUR

Darcy thought she looked quite well, all things considered. She and her sisters were practically living in a hovel in the worst part of London, and they barely had enough room for all of them there. It was a pity. And he knew that she didn't want his help, but he would be damned if he let this continue. This was his fault. Well, at least it was his fault by proxy. He was the one who had proposed to Elizabeth, and he still wasn't even sure why he'd done such a thing.

When he had done it, he had been of two minds about it. He'd been less than complimentary because he wasn't certain of himself. That was why she'd refused him, or so she'd said. But after she had refused him, he had felt better about it all. After all, it was probably better if things continued to stand that way. That was the right way of things. He couldn't marry her. He was meant to marry someone connected.

Of course, he'd had no intention of marrying his cousin Anne. His aunt wished it, and his mother used to joke about it, many years ago, but he didn't take it seriously.

Then the business at Rosings happened.

Darcy hadn't been there. He and Colonel Fitzwilliam had taken their leave of the place, and then his aunt had invited Cumberbottom to visit. Darcy did not know the man well, but the few times he had sat down with the man, Cumberbottom had struck him as a low, leering sort of man. Not the sort of man he'd want near his own sister, for instance.

But then he heard the news, because everyone was talking of it. Cumberbottom had taken Elizabeth aside, purportedly so that he could hear her play the pianoforte, and then the two of them had shared a passionate kiss. Naturally, Cumberbottom had proposed to Elizabeth, but Elizabeth had refused him.

Darcy had chuckled when he heard that. Of course she had refused. That was what she did, after all. Refuse marriage proposals.

But then he realized what this meant for Elizabeth, and he was regretful. As a woman who had kissed another man, she was damaged goods. No one was going to be interested in marrying her now. And her loose morals looked bad for the entire family. It was unfortunate. Especially when Darcy rather blamed Cumberbottom for all of it. He imagined that the fellow had forced the kiss on Elizabeth, who hadn't been interested in kissing him at all. Knowing Elizabeth, he couldn't imagine she was the least bit attracted to Cumberbottom.

Elizabeth was packed off and sent home so that her parents could talk some sense into her and see that she must marry Cumberbottom, for he was still willing to marry her, even after the slight to his pride of her rather public refusal, which had apparently been yelled so loudly that everyone in Rosings had heard it. She had also used some rather colorful language.

That was when Darcy began to suspect something else was afoot. Why was Cumberbottom so eager to marry Elizabeth Bennet, a girl with no fortune and no connections? He'd pulled a nasty trick, but it was the kind of trick usually pulled with heiresses. That was why girls with fortune were guarded within an inch of their lives, so that cads like Cumberbottom couldn't get to them.

Darcy went back to Rosings to speak to his aunt about it.

"Oh," said Lady Catherine when he brought it up. "I

should have known you'd be antsy about that bit of news. I only wish it had gone more smoothly."

"What do you mean?" said Darcy. "Did you have something to do with it?"

"Well, you couldn't expect me to stand idly by while you tried to marry that girl, could you? You are meant for Anne," said Lady Catherine.

"What did you do?" Darcy was angry. He was surprised at how angry he was.

"Well, I simply arranged for Mr. Cumberbottom to propose to Miss Bennet. I can't believe the ungrateful wretch of a girl refused him."

"You bribed him, you mean?" said Darcy. "You bribed him to assault her?"

"Oh, you're so melodramatic," she said.

Darcy gaped at her. "You've ruined her. She was a perfectly lovely girl, and now she's ruined, and for no reason other than the fact that you were worried I might marry her. She refused my proposal."

"The first time," said Lady Catherine. "She was playing coy, trying to determine if you still loved her."

"I assure you, that was not what she was about. She despises me," said Darcy. "You have ruined an innocent girl for no reason at all."

"Well," said his aunt. "Let that be a lesson to you. If you go about proposing willy-nilly to women you're not meant to marry, I shall put a stop to it however I can."

Darcy clenched his jaw. "You can't force me to marry Miss de Bourgh."

"Can't I?"

In the end, she'd had her wish. She'd bullied him into it. One reason was that he'd not met another girl that he liked nearly as much as Elizabeth. Another was the fact that he didn't want his aunt ruining the reputation of any other innocent girl. In the end, he reasoned, marriage was about creating a family, and he already had ties to Anne. No matter he didn't love her. No matter at all.

At the time, he'd strongly considered the idea of a mistress, sometime later, after he'd squared away the business of an heir with Anne, and after the children were a bit older. Then maybe he'd have his dalliances. Then maybe he could have something that resembled love. What was love, anyway, but a short-lived period of infatuation that fed on things like absence and forbidden ardor? Certainly nothing like that could really exist with one's wife, anyway.

But he'd never taken a mistress, and now he had suggested it to Elizabeth, when he hadn't even meant to. He hadn't gone there with that as his objective. It was not the sort of thing he would ask of a lady such as her. Dash it all, he had gone there to save her from such a fate, not to provide it for her. To make her his mistress degraded her. It was the most horrid thing he could have proposed.

But then, he was a horrid man, wasn't he?

He and his aunt didn't speak anymore. Not since Anne's funeral, when Lady Catherine had screamed in his face that he'd killed her only daughter as tears streamed down her face.

Her words had burrowed into his heart like a poison barb. He feared it was all true.

* * *

Elizabeth did not tell Jane what Mr. Darcy had wanted to speak to her alone about. She couldn't. She said that he hemmed and hawed and then seemed to lose his nerve and then hurried out of there as if there was fire on his heels.

"I hear that his wife died," said Jane. "Perhaps he came to propose to you, but our conditions here at home frightened him away. He must know that if he married you, he'd be taking all of us on as well."

"He would never marry me," said Elizabeth. "He thinks me far too low beneath him for that." *He thinks of me as someone who could be his mistress.* Ah, but that wasn't fair. She was the one who had put the idea of her being a mistress in his head. He had not lowered her to that point. She had lowered herself. Anyway, perhaps in a way, it was flattering.

He had wanted to marry her when he proposed, and he must have truly meant that he was attracted to her, because now he seemed to want her still.

Elizabeth moved through the evening chores, thinking about it. She and her sisters cooked for themselves now, and they cleaned up as well. Lydia did not like the way that they lived. She often pointed out that they could save money and they could all live better if everyone went to live with Lydia. But that would mean embracing the fact that their sister was a fallen woman and the destruction that would wreak on the Bennet name. After what Elizabeth had done, they would be hopeless. So, they stayed in their home, and they did the best that they could. Elizabeth would not have minded, she supposed, falling a bit further, since she had already sunk so low.

When she had denied Cumberbottom's offer of marriage, her father had been staunchly in her corner, though her mother was in fits about it. Her father insisted that no daughter of his would be forced to marry a man she found abominable. And Cumberbottom was the worst. He made her skin crawl, the way that he had put his hands and his lips on her. It had been the most horrifying experience of her life. To marry a man who had forced his kisses on her, that was unthinkable.

She was happy that her father had not made her marry him. She was glad of that. But it had consequences. She was damaged goods and her sisters prospects had sunk low. She couldn't move them all into Lydia's house, even if it meant a more comfortable day-to-day life, because they would have no prospects after that. Kitty would probably become a courtesan herself. She had no common sense either. And Mary? Well, Mary might simply fall ill from sheer force of will from the disgust she would feel at the whole family. Heaven knew that Mary still bore a grudge against Elizabeth for not guarding her virtue more carefully.

At any rate, Darcy had come and gone, and now Elizabeth was back in the same situation she had been in before, except she was feeling incredibly stupid for having turned Darcy down. It was her dashed pride, that's what it was. If she had swallowed it all those year ago and married him, think where they would all be now! But no, she had not done it, and now she was too proud to be his mistress?

Why, she was going to become the mistress of this Chivsworth, who she had never met, but who must be somewhat monstrous if he were so picky in his mistresses. Even if he weren't monstrous, he was a stranger, and his touch would not be welcome to her. It would probably be like forcing herself to undergo the caresses of Cumberbottom. Well, no, perhaps not as bad. She wasn't sure. But it *could* be that bad.

And on the other hand, there was Mr. Darcy, who was altogether pleasing to look upon and who had that rumbling dark, deep voice and those ... those *shoulders*, and he was offering, and she had sent him out of the house?

What was she thinking?

His offer was altogether more favorable than the one from Chivsworth.

On the other hand, it would pain her, perhaps more than she could say, to have Mr. Darcy look down upon her so, to be someone who Mr. Darcy paid for services. It was horrible to think of, and she did not think she could bear it. And that was why she had sent him away. Perhaps it didn't make any sense, but there it was.

As the evening wore on, however, Elizabeth grew more and more agitated. Jane inquired what was wrong, and Elizabeth said that she needed to go and see Lydia about something important, a matter of finance. It wasn't usual for Elizabeth to leave in the evening to see Lydia, but it had happened before, so Jane thought nothing of it and said she would make her excuses to their sisters.

Lydia had use of Mr. Farthing's carriage on a rather permanent basis due to friendly relations between the two of them, and Elizabeth made use of it from time to time as well. She called for the carriage, but she did not have it take her to Lydia's home.

Instead, she had the carriage take her to a different part of London altogether. She was about to call on a gentleman alone, and her fate would be quite sealed. No respectable woman did such a thing. She ascended the steps to his door and knocked.

When a footman answered, he seemed a bit shocked to see her there, all alone, but he showed her in to a sitting room and went off to retrieve his master. Elizabeth supposed she was lucky the man of the house was at home and not off somewhere else at a party or ball. After tonight, she would be his mistress. She had made her choice. This was the man to whom she would surrender her virtue. It was all to be settled.

When Mr. Darcy came into the room, she stood.

He was surprised to see her. "Miss Bennet. I had not thought... You are unaccompanied?"

"I don't see that it matters," she said. "Considering what you asked of me earlier."

Mr. Darcy blushed. "Oh, I don't know what came over me." He coughed and looked around the room, out of sorts. "It's not the least like me to say such things to a woman. Any woman, let alone a woman like..." He coughed again. "I say, I had better ask someone to bring up something. Perhaps some cakes or tea or—"

"A strong port?" she said.

He turned to her, eyebrows raised. And then he nodded once, briskly and went to the door to deliver her missive. That done, he came back to sit down opposite her.

There was a fire in the fireplace, cheerily blazing now, although it had just been lit upon Elizabeth's arrival. The room was becoming nicely warmed. She rubbed her hands together briskly.

"Well, to what do I owe the honor of your presence?" he said, smiling at her.

Something in his smile made a shiver run down the back of her neck. It was thrilling and frightening all at once. "Well, I thought about it," she said.

"Thought about what?" he said.

They were interrupted then by a servant who had come with the port.

An interval of some minutes passed until they were each settled with a glass of wine and alone again, no one to listen to their conversation.

"Where were we?" said Mr. Darcy.

"I only thought that I was being ridiculous," she said. "I have always been so with you. I have an exceeding amount of pride, even now, after I have been brought so low. I don't know what it is about you that brings it out of me. But I do need help. My mother's debts are formidable, and they must be seen to, or we will be carted off to prison. And as much as I have survived, I do not know that I could survive that. I think that we might chip away at them with Lydia's help, but I would rather have them settled and done with quickly, and that is why I had agreed to the arrangement with Chivsworth. But I know nothing of him, and I am acquainted with you. And you are…" She swallowed. "Well, if I am going to do it, I find the prospect of it being with you much more amenable than with, um, a stranger. So…" She took a gulp of wine and then looked up at Mr. Darcy to see how he was taking this little speech of hers.

There was something hungry in his gaze as he looked at her, but also something else. Amusement? He found her funny?

She wanted to be angry with him, but she drank more port instead. "Well, say something Mr. Darcy, for heaven's sake."

"I don't know what it is you want me to say," he said. "I

have already told you that I made that offer to you earlier in error. I should never have said something so offensive and improper."

"So, you have rescinded it?" She chuckled bitterly and drained the glass of port. "And here I am making a fool of myself. I should know that you only want me when you are out of your senses."

"Oh, that is not what I meant."

"No?"

"More port?"

"Please."

He got up and refilled her glass from the bottle. Then, he sat back down and gazed into the fire. "You wish me to renew my offer?"

"Not if you do not wish it."

"Oh…" And now he chuckled, ruefully. He studied his knuckles. And when he spoke again, his voice was that gravelly voice from earlier, the one that had cut through her and made her feel undone. "I wish it."

Her breath caught. She gulped at the wine and now she felt lightheaded.

He raised his gaze to hers. "Very well, then. I renew the offer. Be my mistress, Miss Bennet."

She swallowed hard. "All right," and her voice was thin.

"All right," he echoed. He drank his wine and gazed at her with that penetrating look, only this time, it seemed to go straight through her clothes and skin and insides, all the way to her soul.

CHAPTER FIVE

After Elizabeth left, Darcy had to lie down because he'd had far too much to drink. Before she'd arrived and they'd finished off a bottle of port together, he'd been drinking whiskey, and he knew the combination would do him no favors. He'd also behaved rather horribly. Could he blame the drink for the shameful way he'd egged her on?

There was no excuse for it. He could not take advantage of her in this way. To do so made him a villain, just as bad as that Chivsworth fellow, which he hated without knowing. Almost as bad as Wickham, although not quite so bad as that, not really. He would be taking care of Elizabeth, after all, and her sisters, and he wasn't twisting her affections for some material gain. He did care about her.

But, yes, fine, there it was. He would admit it. He wanted to bed her.

Apparently, he wasn't above paying for it.

He would have given her the money regardless, of course. He had already had some of his people making inquiries into the debts incurred by Mrs. Bennet, and they were not formidable to him. He could have them erased in a moment.

But no, there was something perverse in him, and he wanted her first. He would have her, and then he would settle the debts, and then he would pay her triple the amount she asked for on top of that, and he would make sure that she and her sisters could live somewhere better, with decent servants, and… and…

He already felt guilty and he hadn't even touched her.

When he woke up the next morning, his head was aching. Breakfast was cold and Georgiana was playing on her pianoforte, shut up in her room. He knew better than to disturb her when she was engrossed in her music. She wouldn't be angry with him, but she would not hear him. When she was lost to her playing, there was no connecting with her. She would ignore anything he said.

He ate a great deal, anyway. He knew that the best thing for a night of too much drink was a full belly if he could stomach the food, and he could.

After breakfast he went to call on Colonel Fitzwilliam, but the colonel was still abed. It was noon. Darcy shouldn't have expected otherwise, though. That was the way of it with his cousin. He waited, and Colonel Fitzwilliam came down in his banyan, his hair in disarray, about a quarter hour later.

"Join me for breakfast, Darcy," said Colonel Fitzwilliam.

"I've already eaten," said Darcy, but he sat at the table while his cousin ate.

"I haven't seen you in days," said Fitzwilliam. "I thought you were here in town to find Miss Darcy a husband. You realize that she has to be seen by prospective husbands for such an event to occur?"

"Yes, of course," said Darcy. "And I shall be bringing her out to some more balls soon enough. She is so dreadfully shy, you know."

"I do, but she is a lovely creature. I'm sure once she overcomes her shyness, it will not be long before she meets the right man."

"I would like her settled," said Darcy. "I worry about her future happiness."

"And you, out of mourning," said Fitzwilliam. "You must be on the prowl as well."

"I think not," said Darcy. "Actually, I came to speak to you about something. To ask for advice."

"Oh, advice from me? Darcy wants advice from me? This is quite a shock."

Darcy sighed. " I do value your opinion about some things."

" I had no inkling that you did, I must confess. You are marvelously skilled at hiding your admiration of me." The colonel grinned and then filled his mouth with buttered toast.

"I am thinking of taking a mistress."

The colonel chewed his toast and swallowed. " Well, good for you. I wouldn't know a thing about it. I can't afford a mistress."

" You are always gallivanting with women of questionable morals."

"Yes, whores," said Fitzwilliam. "Much easier. You can pay them for a night and then wash your hands of them in the morning. A mistress? A mistress is just like having a wife, except you spend all your time trying not to get her with child instead of the other way around."

Darcy blanched. How could he have not thought about that?

Fitzwilliam continued. " You have to clothe them and give them money and pay for their living quarters, and all for what? So, that you can do with them the exact same things that you do with your wife? Just get married again, Darcy."

"I don't want to get married," Darcy said darkly. "And I don't want to get anyone with child."

Fitzwilliam was quiet. He regarded the remaining piece of toast on his plate, but he did not pick it up. Seconds ticked by. "Listen, what happened to Mrs. Darcy and the baby, that was—"

"We don't have to discuss it," said Darcy.

"You'll have to get married eventually," said Fitzwilliam.

"No, I won't," said Darcy. "I don't have to do anything I don't want to do."

"So, who will inherit Pemberley, then? That fat cousin of yours on your father's side? Can you imagine what he'd do to the place?"

"I plan to outlive him," said Darcy, sighing. "No, I don't know. I shall wait on all that. Perhaps someday, I shall find a very sturdy-looking woman. One with enormous hips and large hands. One not likely to succumb. But... no, not until Georgiana is settled."

"So, in the meantime, while you wait for this sturdy woman, you want to cavort with a woman who is a bit more lovely, and you immediately thought you would like to take a mistress?"

"I..." Darcy sighed. "You know, perhaps I have not really thought it through."

"You have not," said Fitzwilliam, reaching for his cup of tea. "Trust me on this, what you want are whores. I even know a place where you can find all manner of extremely winsome girls. Come with me some night, and the two of us—"

"No," said Darcy. "That's all right. Thank you, though, cousin." He stood up from the table. "I shan't take up anymore of your breakfast."

"You're leaving already?" called the colonel.

Darcy bowed slightly at the door.

"Do tell me the next time you and Georgiana will be out and about," called the colonel after him.

Darcy was shown out by a footman and then went back to his home, where a servant was waiting with a letter for him from Elizabeth.

His stomach turned over. What had she written to say? Had she called it all off? He felt relief and disappointment in equal measure.

But instead, he found inside a rather business-like letter detailing all the things that Elizabeth was putting into place for the two of them to enter into this arrangement of theirs. She said that she was ordering dresses and renting a house and procuring a few servants and that all these things would be billed to him. She estimated that she would be ready to receive him for the first time in about a week. She signed off politely, but there was no warmth in the letter at all.

Well, he supposed that she must be somewhat accustomed to this sort of thing, given what she arranged with her sister. But still, he felt unsure of all of this.

What had he gotten himself into?

* * *

"You mustn't expect much from the first time, Lizzy," said Lydia, lounging in the parlor at her home.

Elizabeth was standing in the midst of several swaths of fabric and lace, all in light colors of violets, blues, yellows, and white. She had helped Lydia secure clothing for all these years, but she found it was rather different to be doing it for herself. She wasn't going overboard with the clothes she was having made. She didn't need too much, just a modest wardrobe. She wasn't sure that Mr. Darcy would want to take her out at all, although many men did like to be seen with their mistresses, and she couldn't imagine that Mr. Darcy would be different. However, she had only commissioned three evening dresses, which she would wear to receive him if he chose to keep her at home.

She would be residing at this new home during the time that they were interacting. She couldn't very well have Mr. Darcy come to visit her where she lived with her sisters, and it wouldn't be proper for her to live at his house. Staying with Lydia would be awkward as well, so there was really nothing for it. She must have her own house.

She assumed it would be a temporary arrangement, but it was rather nice. She was looking forward to having a maid to dress her and fix her hair. She was looking forward to having a staff to cook meals and the like. She needed to have that for the nights that Mr. Darcy would dine with her. He must be entertained in the style to which he was accustomed.

"I am not expecting anything," said Elizabeth, but that

was also a lie. She had been thinking quite a bit about Mr. Darcy's bare shoulders lately, she had to admit. She had not ever seen a man's shoulders unclothed, not in real life, but she had seen statues and paintings, and she was quite able to picture what he might look like. He had exceedingly broad shoulders, and she could see that he was muscled under his jacket and shirt and cravat, and she had a feeling that his shoulders would be rather pleasant to look at.

In fact, most recently, she was given to a fantasy in which Mr. Darcy was telling her to get into bed in his very, very deep voice, and he was not wearing a shirt at all when he did so. The fantasy made her feel very shivery and it also made things inside her quite taut and coiled up. She wasn't sure, not exactly, but she thought that if she found a release of that coiled-up feeling, it would be exceptionally pleasant.

Lydia sat up, a look of alarm on her face. "Oh, dear, Lizzy. I had thought you hated Mr. Darcy. Isn't he a horrible man? You did refuse his marriage proposal, did you not? I thought he was snobby and priggish. I thought you had only accepted the offer of being his mistress because he was marginally better than Chivsworth. But you are in love with Mr. Darcy."

Elizabeth stood up straight, knocking fabric and lace askew. "I most certainly am not!"

"Oh, you are." Lydia got off the lounge she had been lying on. "This will not do, Lizzy."

"I'm not in love with him."

"You must not be in love," said Lydia. "It will ruin it all. You will be hurt. And you might get jealous at some point. This is a disaster."

"It's not a disaster, because I am not in love with him."

"Listen," said Lydia. "Here's what you'll have to do. Tell him no kissing on the lips."

"What?" said Elizabeth. "I don't even know why that would—"

"It will be easier," said Lydia. "Kissing is intimate. It's

romantic. You take that out of the equation, and it's all about his body and your body and nothing else. It will protect you. Mark my words, Lizzy, you must do that."

Elizabeth shook her head. "I am not in love with him," she said again, but her voice sounded pathetic, even to her.

"Maybe it will all be fine, anyway," said Lydia. "Your first night with him will be a disappointment, so then that may cool your ardor toward him."

"Why do you say that?"

"Because it's always disappointing," said Lydia. "It will hurt, for one thing. And there may be blood."

"I know all about this," said Elizabeth, sitting back down amongst her fabrics. "You have told me of it before."

"And men—all men—are frightfully stupid about women's bodies. They are too rough and clumsy and they are not the least bit skilled at giving a woman pleasure."

Elizabeth picked up some lace and began to fold it. "Well, I am not expecting pleasure. It is only important that he find pleasure."

"Most men like it better if they think you're enjoying it as well," said Lydia. "Which means that a woman has two choices."

"Oh? What are they?"

"Either feign pleasure or find ways to make the pleasure real."

"How does one make it real?"

"Well, you must learn your own body, first," said Lydia. "Once you know what brings you pleasure, you can show men how to touch you."

"Oh, I could not." Elizabeth blushed. "Tell him what to do? He would never—"

"He would love it," said Lydia, shrugging. "They all do. Men are stupid when it comes to this sort of thing, trust me. They are big, dumb clumsy sweaty things who need to be led around by the prick."

"Lydia!" Elizabeth blushed and laughed and hurled the

lace at her sister.

Who laughed as well. "Was it the word that bothered you?"

"No, it's only that you…" Elizabeth buried her head in her hands.

"You're going to be up close and personal with one soon enough, Lizzy. Might as well come to terms with that."

Elizabeth swallowed hard. What had she gotten herself into?

CHAPTER SIX

Darcy coughed. He had come into the bedchamber in this house of Elizabeth's, and it was dark in here. The only light was the lantern he had brought with him. He would have liked a bit more light. He wanted to see her while this happened, after all.

He could not believe things had already progressed so far. The week that she had told him she would need to prepare things had passed quickly, and then she had summoned him to the house for dinner, and for… well, consummation, he supposed.

Dinner had been an exercise in torture. She was nervous, and he could tell. She kept alternating between being frightfully quiet and then babbling about nothing. She had gone on a ten-minute tirade about the weather in London, pronouncing it insupportable.

She'd barely eaten.

He hadn't either.

He wasn't sure, but he thought that perhaps things should go a bit differently between them. This was all putting him in mind of the awkwardness of his wedding night, and he wanted something different with a mistress. Mistresses were supposed to allow men to give in to their desires, after all. It was not supposed to be the way it was with a wife, who was stiff and quiet and unmoving.

But as he made his way closer to the bed, he saw Elizabeth, and she was lying flat on the bed, clutching the covers up to her chin. Her dark hair was splayed out on the pillow behind her. Her eyes were wide. She was utterly lovely. And utterly terrified.

Dash it all.

He wasn't going to do this again. It was one thing with Anne. She had a duty, and so did he, and he felt that he could get through the act because he was required to do so. He didn't think she'd gotten much out of it, but that was the way of things when people were married, at least that was what Darcy was given to understand. There was congress between a man and a wife—which was a formal sort of thing—and then there was congress with a mistress, which he was *paying* for, and he was not going to do all of that again.

Because, truly, he had not enjoyed what amounted to… to forcing his wife. Not forcing. She was willing. She hadn't attempted to stop him. But she only lay there, staring up at him with her frightened eyes, flinching occasionally, which compelled him to squeeze his eyes closed and think of other things. God help him. To think of Elizabeth Bennet.

What was he supposed to think of if Elizabth was actually with him and she was gazing up at him in that same terrified way? There was no other fantasy he could turn to. He didn't spend a lot of time engaging with fleshly thoughts, anyway, not since he was a youth. He had other things to worry about these days. He didn't dally in adolescent fantasy.

Elizabeth sat up in the bed. She was wearing a shift, nothing beneath it, at least as far as he could see. Her unbound hair was so beautiful it made his breath catch in his throat. "What?"

He had stopped in the middle of the room, just frozen here, and she must wonder what was wrong. He squared his shoulders. "I'm not sure…" He didn't know how to continue.

" Aren't you going to remove your clothing? " said Elizabeth.

He let out a low chuckle. " Are you even aware of

what..." He had no words for this. He made vague gestures with his hands. "What it is that is to happen," he settled on.

"Of course," said Elizabeth. "I know of all of it." She drew in a shaky breath. "I don't understand why you're simply standing there. Hadn't we better get on with it?"

Anne had known nothing of the enterprise, at least that was how it had seemed to him. They hadn't really spoken. It had all been a wordless, awkward encounter. And they'd somehow managed to get away with only doing it once before Anne was increasing. He didn't want to repeat all of that, and he didn't want to continue thinking of his dead wife.

"I..." He squared his shoulders. "That is, I am not exactly in the frame of mind for it right now."

"One needs to be in a certain frame of mind?" Elizabeth looked concerned. "I did not know of that."

"Perhaps not every man is like me," said Darcy, coming to sit on the bed, bowing his head. "Perhaps the sight of you in that shift with your hair down would be enough for someone else... perhaps it *should* be enough."

"But it isn't?" She looked down at herself. "Is there something wrong with me? Do I not please you?"

"It is..." He cleared his throat. "Well, you don't seem particularly eager at the prospect of it. I suppose that is what is making it difficult for me."

She considered this. "Well, I cannot lie. I am not. My sister fed me full of horror stories before I arrived. Pain and blood and how I should not kiss you on the mouth and—"

"What?" He was insistent. "You will kiss me if I wish you to kiss me. That is preposterous. I am not paying for all this to be denied kissing." He gestured around the house.

She gathered up the sheets and clutched them to her chest. "All right," she said softly.

"Pain?" he said. "So, it is to hurt you?"

"My sister said so," said Elizabeth.

"Hang it all," said Darcy, getting up from the bed. "I'm

not doing this."

"What?" said Elizabeth, sounding somewhat panicked. "But you must. You have to."

"I do not have to do anything," said Darcy. "I don't find the prospect of causing you pain particularly erotic. Forgive me for that." He was sarcastic.

She climbed out of bed. "Mr. Darcy, please—"

"If you're worried about the money, I was going to help you anyway. I had already decided on it. I don't know why I agreed to all of this. I was drunk when you came to my house that night, and I had quite lost my head. I can never have a mistress. It's… it's intolerable."

"You *have* a mistress," said Elizabeth. "I am right here. And what you need to do is to remove your clothing so that we can do this thing now. I have been working myself up for this all day, and I will have it over with as soon as possible."

"No," said Darcy.

"I won't take money from you that's charity," she said. "I have far too much pride—"

"And that is your downfall, madam."

"Oh, it's mine, is it?" She shot him a pointed look.

"I think this Chivsworth must be a villain," Darcy muttered to himself. "Because to want to bed a virgin, it seems… despicable."

"Why? Have you bedded many virgins?" Elizabeth said, and the fear had surfaced in her voice, causing it warble.

"Just my wife."

She sucked an audible breath and she sat back down on the bed. "Oh," she said in a different voice.

He probably should not have mentioned that he had been married, should he have? It was not the sort of thing that women liked to know about, other women. But she had asked, damn it.

"And what was it like?" Elizabeth whispered.

"Horrible," he said. "I won't do it again."

"Well…" Elizabeth's voice sounded a bit stronger.

"Perhaps if you just endeavored to be gentle, it wouldn't be so bad. Do you think you could do that?"

"No, this is not going to happen between us, Miss Bennet. It cannot. I am incapable of it."

"How could you be incapable?" She got back up and came to him. She took him by the shoulders.

He tensed at her touch.

She looked into his eyes. "You are not wounded or disfigured or something?"

"I am not aroused," he said.

She looked at him blankly.

"I thought you said that you knew how this was to work," he said.

"Yes," she said.

"So? Explain it to me." Now, he was being horrible to her, but he didn't care.

She blushed, and it made her even prettier. "You... the, er, man puts his member betwixt the woman's thighs, all the way inside... her."

"Yes, well, you're missing a key step there," he said.

"I am?"

"The man's member needs to be..." He foundered. "Stiff."

Her eyes widened. "Okay, yes. I think I have just now belatedly gotten the joke in a number of plays." She cleared her throat. "Yours isn't?"

"No."

"Why not? Can we make it that way?"

He almost wanted to laugh. He almost wanted to kiss her. Seize her and pull her against him and run his hands through her hair, and then maybe he *would* be aroused, maybe...

But no. He wanted no part of another encounter with a frightened woman. He felt guilty about having put her in this position at all. The fact that things were not going smoothly between them, it was a sign that it was never meant to be in the first place.

So, he turned on his heel and quit the room without answering her.

*　*　*

Elizabeth waited a long time in the room, expecting him to return. When he didn't, she dressed without the help of her maid, so a bit sloppily, and then went to search for him.

She found him the room she had prepared especially for him, in case he should want some time to himself when they were together. It had a desk for letter writing, and some books and a few chairs near the fireplace. She really had quite enjoyed outfitting the place for the two of them. It was as though she had been pretending that they were to have some kind of relationship, she supposed, as though he was to be her husband, even though she knew it would not be that way at all.

He was sitting by the fire with a glass of whiskey in his hand.

She crossed the room to sit down next to him. "Mr. Darcy." She reached over, boldly, and put her hand on his thigh. "I am sorry. This is my fault. Lydia had explained to me that men enjoy the act more if they are with a woman who is enjoying herself. I am sorry if I did not seem eager, but I quite am. I want this." She wasn't lying either. Some part of her did want it. She was frightened, but she was also excited, and she was rather disappointed not have seen his bare shoulders. She wondered if they were the way that she had imagined them.

He looked up at her. "Don't be ridiculous, Miss Bennet."

"Am I being ridiculous?"

"There is no fault to assign." He gently plucked her hand off of his thigh and placed it in her own lap.

For some reason, this hurt her. She wasn't sure why, but she straightened her spine and drew in a breath.

"I never wanted this," he said. "Not truly. You are not the sort of woman who is to be entered into an arrangement such as this with. I could not live with myself if I treated you with such a lack of respect."

She was quiet for a moment. "Well, then, I suppose you are breaking things between us."

"I want to help—"

"I shall simply have to go to Mr. Chivsworth," she said, even though she was unsure she would have the strength to do such a thing.

He got up out of his chair, sloshing his drink all over the carpet. "You wouldn't dare."

She gazed up at him. "You have no hold on me. You cannot tell me—"

"I will settle your mother's debts. And I will continue to pay for this house, but you must move your sisters in and—"

"No," she said.

"How can your pride allow you to… to *spread your legs* for a man but not to accept my help?" His face was red, and he was sputtering.

"I don't know," she said. "But I can't take money for nothing, Mr. Darcy. It doesn't seem right."

"You will not go to Mr. Chivsworth," he said. "I will not have another man's hands on you."

She raised her eyebrows. "You seem rather possessive of someone that you claim you never wanted."

"What?" He looked her over. "I never said I didn't want you."

"You did. Just moments ago. You said you never wanted this, and that I was not the sort of woman—"

"I never wanted to make a whore of you!" he snapped.

She recoiled from him.

He winced. He turned away. "I'm apologize, Miss Bennet. That is not what you are, and I am sorry that I… Hang everything." He down the rest of his drink, set the glass on the mantle and started across the room.

"You can't walk out on me again!" she cried.

He stopped. He turned to look at her. "I do want you. Of course I want you. Would I have agreed to all of this if I didn't?"

"Then…" She swallowed. "Take me, Mr. Darcy."

"I cannot," he said. "Not like this. Not…" He sank both of his hands into his hair. It was quiet. Then he dropped his hands and looked at her. "All right, listen. The arrangement stands. You remain here. You are mine. You don't go anywhere near Chivsworth. And maybe … maybe with time…" He cleared his throat. "In the meantime, you will accompany me to balls to dance with me so that I don't have to dance with strangers."

"Balls?" She knew that she might be called upon to do so, but it seemed he had brought it up out of nowhere.

"If you are worried about being recognized, we can stick to masquerades, at least to begin with. Georgiana finds it easier to dance when she has the barrier of a mask, so that is all well and good."

"I don't see why you would need me as a dance partner. Certainly, there are many women who—"

"I don't like dancing with people I don't know. I thought I had told you this before."

"Oh, yes," she said. "I remember now. We spoke of it at Rosings once, did we not?"

He inclined his head.

That all seemed like another life. And the thought of Rosings brought back bad memories for her. She shook that all away. "Well, if you are always dancing with me, people will notice. They'll think—"

"I don't give a damn what they think," he said. "I am going to balls only to try to find my sister a husband. You assist me in that manner, and you will be providing me a service, for which I shall pay you handsomely. And all is settled between us, then."

She considered. "Well, I suppose that is true."

"Good." He turned and started again for the door.

"Mr. Darcy?"

He stopped and turned again. "What?" He sounded a bit exasperated.

"You're leaving then?" She wished she didn't sound so disappointed.

"Yes. Good night, Miss Bennet."

"Good night, Mr. Darcy."

And he was gone.

Later, she climbed back into her cold, lonely bed. She wasn't much accustomed to sleeping alone. She wondered why she felt so acutely unfinished as she tossed and turned herself to sleep.

* * *

"It was wretched," said Elizabeth. "I couldn't believe he refused me."

"I admit," Lydia said, surveying the dresses that they had draped out over the bed in her room, "it is most odd. I've never heard of a gentleman behaving in such a way."

Elizabeth ran her fingers over a red dress. "This one, perhaps?"

"Yes, you should try it on," said Lydia. "It is a Cleopatra costume. There is a wig that goes with it somewhere. I never wore it. No one will associate it with me." It was a tricky thing, borrowing costumes from her sister, considering that Lydia was so notorious. Her costumes were the stuff of gossip. Sometimes they were even written about in the papers.

Elizabeth would have had new ones commissioned, but she knew that Lydia had some costumes that had never been worn, and she wanted the excuse to talk to her sister, besides. She had to admit that Lydia knew better about these sorts of things.

Elizabeth picked up the dress. "I shall try it on. Yes." She called for her maid, Meggy, who had accompanied her here to Lydia's house. Meggy was a bit scandalized by it all, as if she hadn't realized that she was employed by a woman of questionable reputation to begin with. As Meggy helped Elizabeth out of her dress, Elizabeth sighed. "Well, what did I do wrong? I know that I shouldn't have admitted that I wasn't eager for it. You told me as much. Did I do anything else to ruin it?"

"That's the thing," said Lydia, sitting down on a couch and throwing back her head. "It sounds to me as if you *are* eager for it. It's as I said before. You're in love with him."

"Oh, stop it," said Elizabeth.

"What's more, I think he's in love with you," said Lydia.

"What?" Elizabeth turned to her sharply, causing Meggy to yell at her to hold still. Elizabeth apologized and allowed the maid to help her into the red dress. "He's not in love with me. He refused me. He finds some fault in me, undoubtedly. I don't know what it is, but something."

"I don't think so," said Lydia. "I think he cares about your comfort. That's what you said. He didn't want to hurt you. It's rather nice, actually." She sighed. "Your Mr. Darcy is a bit gallant, isn't he? He'd be one of those chivalrous knights in the stories."

" How does his refusing me make him gallant? " Elizabeth snorted. Meggy worked at the buttons on the dress.

"Well, if you can't see it, I don't know if I can explain it to you," said Lydia. "Anyway, you mustn't worry about it. He'll get over it, I think. He'll be overcome, and he won't be able to resist you, and… oh, I think it might work out very nicely for you, Lizzy. I imagine he might take care of you for the rest of your life. And if you have children, he might even provide for them, and—"

"No!" said Elizabeth, horrified. "I couldn't do that. I couldn't have bastard children. To bring children into the world with no father, no future? That would be horrid."

"That's what I am saying. He would likely claim them and take care of them."

Elizabeth furrowed her brow, quiet as Meggy worked at the dress. She didn't like the picture that Lydia was creating.

Part of her did. She couldn't deny that she was saddened at the thought she would never have children. And she thought Mr. Darcy would make a good father. Having children with him was not a repugnant thought, not in the least. But to have them as his mistress, it wasn't the same. Besides which, Mr. Darcy would eventually have to get married again, and then… Elizabeth felt as if she couldn't breathe. "This dress is far too tight!" she gasped.

"No, I think it fits you nicely," countered Meggy. "Very flattering if I do say so myself."

Elizabeth looked in the mirror at herself. The dress was actually rather flattering. It was a bit lower at the bodice than she was used to, and her bosom was on display, but it wasn't any more revealing than dresses that other women of good breeding wore. She didn't look like a courtesan, not entirely. She turned this way and that. All right, well, she supposed she did look like a courtesan, a bit, anyway. The thing was, she rather liked the way she looked. She smiled at her reflection.

"That looks lovely on you," said Lydia, who was up and behind her, peering over her shoulder. "I think you must wear that one."

"I agree," said Elizabeth, turning to her sister and smiling.

Lydia smiled back. "Lizzy, I know it isn't ideal, but it's the best a woman in our circumstance could hope for. A long arrangement with a man where he cares for you forever? It is security. And you care for him, so I don't see why you wouldn't want that."

"I intended for it to be temporary between us," Elizabeth said softly.

"Did you discuss that with him? Did you put perimeters on it?"

"Well … no." Elizabeth turned back to look at her reflection. "It would be easier if he would not have refused me. I am sure of it."

"I don't know if that's true," said Lydia.

"You said that you thought he would be with me eventually, that he would be overcome?"

"I do think so, yes."

"Well, the sooner the better," said Elizabeth.

* * *

It was late and Elizabeth was pacing the room in her house. She had sent a note to Mr. Darcy to come and visit her, and she had resolved that she would be eager and willing this time, and that she would do whatever it took to render him capable of being with her, and that it would happen. She needed it to happen. She wasn't sure why she wanted it so, but she was sure that it would make things easier once it was taken care of.

She felt as though she was hovering on a precipice here, living as a mistress but still unenjoyed. She found she had a newfound appreciation for the monologue in *Romeo and Juliet,* when Juliet was waiting for Romeo on their wedding night.

But it was late now, and Darcy had not appeared.

She worried that he would not come, and she did not know if she could bear the sting of another rejection. She told herself that she should not have planned it thus. She should have made sure that he was free to come and see her. He could have some pressing engagement which was keeping her from him.

In the grand scheme of things, it wasn't even that late. Elizabeth knew that balls and parties often went into the wee hours of the morning.

When she was younger, indeed, she remembered the balls she had attended in Hertfordshire, and she and her family were often out quite late then.

Now, why it was barely midnight. If she was to be a courtesan, a lady of the night, she would have to keep later hours.

But she was yawning.

She rang for some tea and drank it sitting by the window, looking for his carriage to come up the street.

She would wait for him, and he would come. He had to.

CHAPTER SEVEN

Darcy stood in the doorway, waiting until the last strains of the piece that Georgiana was playing on the piano were sounded. Before she began to play another, he cleared his throat loudly.

Georgiana, who had not realized that he was even there, jumped, letting out a tiny squeal.

Darcy laughed. "I apologize."

She got up from the piano. "What are you doing here?"

"I wanted to speak to you," he said. "I was going to speak to you at dinner, but you did not come down."

"Oh, yes," said Georgiana, flushing a little. She was a small, delicate girl. He thought she was beautiful, but she did have a bit of an odd look about her sometimes. She could not always look another person in the eye and she seemed out of sorts when it came to trying to converse with others, even those in her family. When she did talk, all she seemed to ever talk of was music. She was consumed by it. "I was working on a new piece."

"Yes, I realize. You've been playing the same thing all afternoon."

"I keep making a mistake," she said. "I can't figure out how to correct it."

"It sounded perfect to me."

"Well, it wasn't." She looked at him in the eye when she said that. "It was flawed, marred. If I could just—"

"Wait," he said. "I didn't come to speak to you about the music."

"Of course you didn't." Her shoulders slumped. "You're going to talk to me about balls again, aren't you?"

"That is the entire reason we came to town," he said. "You are out in society, and you must attend balls and dance with eligible young men and find a husband."

She cringed. "Oh, why must you always bring this up?"

"Because it is what you should be concerned with now."

She sat down at the piano bench and let her fingers roam over the keys.

"Georgiana, please do not start playing again."

"I'm not. It's just, I think better this way. I'm not sure why. But I can find words I can't always find." She paused. "I have been thinking that perhaps I don't want to get married."

"What?" he said. "Of course you want to get married. Everyone wants to get married."

"I don't," she said. "I think it would be a marvelous distraction from playing the pianoforte."

"Distraction from...?" He cleared his throat. "Listen, young ladies cultivate themselves in order to find a husband. They do not allow their pursuits to eclipse their true duties in life."

"It's only that the only thing that I really enjoy doing is playing," said Georgiana. "I don't like talking to people. I don't like dancing. I don't like throwing parties. I don't think I would make a very good wife. And I really don't want to have any babies."

"What do you mean you don't want to have babies? All women want..." He didn't even finish the sentence.

"Well, it doesn't sound at all pleasant," said Georgiana. "I hear that women get ill, and then it's very uncomfortable to have such a round belly, and then it's very painful to bring the babes into the world, not to mention..." Her voice dropped. "Dangerous."

Darcy swallowed.

The silence hovered in the air between them.

All Darcy could hear was the echo of Anne's cries, coming back to him over the months and weeks, the way she had been in so much pain, the way she had sounded so scared.

Would he sentence his sister to that? She was even more delicate than Anne was. What if it went badly for her?

And what was it all for, anyway? Georgiana didn't need a husband for monetary support. She was quite secure with her inheritance. It was only that he felt that she needed someone to look after her, and he thought she would want to be on her own. She couldn't remain under his roof forever. She was a grown woman. She needed to start her own life.

He swallowed again. "We'll discuss this later. But know that you are going to the masquerade ball that we spoke of. There will be no getting out of it, not even if you are ill." Georgiana had the tendency to fake illnesses to get out of going to balls. He didn't trust what she said anymore.

"But Fitzwilliam!" she protested. "I told you I didn't want to go."

"You must," he said. "That is all." He took his leave of her.

There was silence for a few moments and then the piano began again.

He strode down the hallway.

"Sir?" called the butler.

He stopped. "Yes, Mr. Barnes. What can I do for you?"

"This letter was delivered for you this afternoon," said Mr. Barnes, handing him a folded note.

Darcy saw Elizabeth's handwriting, and he felt his heart skip time.

* * *

"Miss Bennet," a voice was saying.

Elizabeth snapped awake, looking about. She had fallen asleep in her chair, holding her empty tea cup. How embarrassing. The housekeeper was bending over her, looking concerned. Elizabeth smoothed at her hair. "I, um, I must have fallen asleep."

"Yes," said the housekeeper, taking her tea cup from her. "Mr. Darcy is here."

"He came!" Elizabeth's heart leapt. She had quite given up on him.

"He is in the sitting room. Do you wish to go down to him?"

"Show him into the bedroom," said Elizabeth, standing up. She was already dressed for bed, with her night jacket over her shift. Her hair was braided, but he had said something before about her hair being down, about finding that pleasing, so as she waited for him to come up, she deftly undid the braid and let her hair fall around her shoulders.

And then he was there, standing in the doorway.

She hurried over to him. "Mr. Darcy, I had thought perhaps you weren't coming."

He looked her over, and he got that look in his eyes again, the piercing one that seemed to penetrate her.

She could hardly breathe. Forcing herself to be brave, she stepped even closer, so that there was naught but inches between them. "I have been thinking that I want to show you that I am eager for—"

He reached out and took a lock of her hair between his thumb and forefinger.

Her voice stopped.

They stood that way for a few moments. He fingered her hair, and she only breathed.

Finally, she found her voice again, and it was breathy and affected. "I want us to be together. Tonight. I asked you here for that reason."

He let his fingers go through her hair, all the way the tips of it, and then he let the lock fall. "Oh, Miss Bennet, I..."

She closed the remaining distance between them, pressing her body against his. Oh! He was warm, even through his clothes. "Please," she whispered.

He rested his forehead against hers. "I... you know that I

do not wish to hurt you."

"My sister says it is only the first time, and that there can be pleasure thereafter. It is simply a fact of the initial encounter, and if we were to get it over with... and if you were to be careful and patient and gentle, I think... I do want it. I do want you."

He shut his eyes.

"Say yes," she said. "And I shall do whatever is necessary to make sure that you are... are..." What was the word he'd used? "Aroused," she finally remembered.

He groaned softly. And then he raised his head and pressed his lips against her forehead. "I don't think that it would take much for that."

"Then? You will?"

He pulled away from her and looked into her eyes. "I don't know that I am in the right frame of mind for it tonight either."

"Truly?" She was disappointed. He had seemed different. And the way his lips had felt against the skin of her forehead, it had been divine. She liked him close, as well.

He cupped her cheek with one hand.

She sighed, shutting her eyes. That was very nice.

"I don't have the proper associations with... with this sort of intimacy, I'm afraid."

She opened her eyes, searching his expression. "I don't know what you mean."

"I had a conversation with my sister tonight, and it reminded me of... of my wife's death."

"Oh," she said, feeling deflated. He had spoken of his wife before. He must have loved her very much. Elizabeth must only be a pale shadow compared to the emotion he'd had for the woman he'd sworn to spend his life with.

"You know that she died giving birth to... to my daughter," he said.

"I..." She shook her head. "I assumed it must be something like that. Or perhaps an illness. She was not strong, Miss de Bourgh. I mean, Mrs. Darcy. I mean—"

"It's fine, yes, to call her by her maiden name. I know who you mean. And no, she wasn't strong. Perhaps that is why I should never have..." He moved away from her, further into the room.

She followed him.

He moved like a lost man, fighting his way through a storm. When he finally reached the bed, he sank down on it and he hung his head.

She sat down next to him. Tentatively, she put a hand on his shoulder. It was firm and solid and large, but perhaps she shouldn't be thinking about such things at a time like this.

"I killed her," he murmured.

"Mr. Darcy, no!" she said, tightening her hand on his shoulder. "That is preposterous. You did no such thing."

"I am the one who got her with child, and she died attempting to bring the child into the world, so it seems to me—"

"Well, you *had* to get her with child. You had no choice. It is what people *do* when they get married. And besides, you must have an heir." Of course, it had been a girl. But Elizabeth decided there was no reason to say anything about that.

"You wish me to be with you," he said. "And that means that there could be a risk that you would..."

She turned away. The thought of children made her uncomfortable too.

"Even if I could give you pleasure when I bedded you, I could not bear it if you were harmed, if you were *killed*—"

"That won't happen!"

"It could happen. It happens every day." His voice broke. "You don't know what it was like, hearing her scream the way she did. I hear it sometimes, in my dreams, and I am so helpless. There is nothing I can do for her, and I can't take it back. I can't take the child out of her. If only I could, but I cannot."

She wrapped her arms around him. "Mr. Darcy, you punish yourself for no reason. You must stop."

He turned to look at her, and there were unshed tears in his eyes.

She clung to him tighter. "It was not your fault," she whispered. "It was *not*."

He turned in her arms, resting his head against her chest, against the swell of her bosom. She tightened her grip on him, and his arms came around her, and his broad shoulders shook for a moment.

And then they fell back on the bed together, and she clutched him to her as closely as she could.

CHAPTER EIGHT

Morning light stole in the room, waking Elizabeth. She had slept in Mr. Darcy's arms, or perhaps he had slept in hers. They were both still in all their clothes, but they were a tangle of legs and arms, and she was close enough that she could feel his breath against her skin. She let out a little hum of satisfaction. There was something perfect about it. She didn't quite know what, but she adored this feeling.

Slowly, she disengaged enough to move so that she was propped up on an elbow, looking down on him.

His eyes were closed, and he was lovely to look upon. Splayed out next to her, his body was strong and firm. His face was relaxed and there was none of the pride that sometimes marked his countenance. He was a very handsome man.

Her hand darted out to caress his cheek, almost of its own volition. She was startled to find the faint prickle of stubble there. It made her smile.

His eyes fluttered open.

"Good morning," she said softly.

" Good morning, " he said. " What are you smiling about?"

"I…" She smiled wider. "I don't know. I suppose I'm happy."

He reached up and wound his hand behind her neck and pulled her down to him. His lips pressed against hers.

Stars burst behind her closed eyelids. Kissing him was like a sweet explosion. She clung to him and pressed close, as close as she could get.

His hand smoothed down her neck and over her spine. She was wearing only her bed jacket and shift, and his touch sent shivers running through her. She gasped.

He pulled away, smiling at her. "You were kind to me last night."

"Of course."

"I don't think I deserve it. I think I have treated you abominably, making you my mistress. It is unforgivable."

"I forgive you," she said. "Besides, you have tried to get out of it repeatedly, and I don't seem to be able to allow you to do so."

He brushed her hair away from her face.

She let out that little satisfied hum again.

He traced the outline of her jaw with one finger and then let it travel over her neck and down to her collarbone.

She was awash in tiny little thrills. She gasped.

"You are beautiful, Miss Bennet. Have I told you this before? The most beautiful creature I think I have ever beheld."

His words made her shudder.

They were kissing again, and it was wonderful.

She could kiss him forever, she decided. They could kiss for eternity, and that would be quite all right with her. She would not mind it in the slightest.

He broke the kiss.

She let out a tiny sigh of protest.

"You truly want this?" he said, and his voice was deep and affected. "You want to be with me?"

She nodded. "I know there are ways to prevent the creation of babes, if that is what troubles you. It troubles me too, in fact. My sister has told me of something, a French letter, I believe it is called. I can procure those if that is what you wish."

"Right, of course," he said. "Yes, I suppose that is a bit of protection." He rolled onto his back and he was no longer touching her.

Had she said something wrong?

"It is only…" His hands scrabbled at his neck, loosening his cravat. "Lord, it is the very devil having slept in one's clothes."

"Oh, I am sorry about that," she said. "I should have, um…" What? Undressed him? She blushed and couldn't help a smile at the thought.

He tore the cravat off, sitting up in the bed. "I am not sure about all of this. There is still risk, even with the French letter, and there is the manner of honor and…"

"You said with time," she said. "So, after the masquerade, then."

He eyed her. "Perhaps."

* * *

Wickham was eating grapes in bed, completely naked, while Lydia was lying next to him, similarly unclothed. She kept snatching the grapes from him before he got them to his mouth and laughing.

"Stop that, Lyddie," he chided her. "You are often inspired by the devil, upon my word."

"And you love it," said Lydia, giggling as she popped a grape she had stolen into her mouth.

"No, I don't," objected Wickham.

"Oh, you do, you do." Lydia rolled away, out of his grasp.

Because he was going to reach for her and tickle her until she apologized. But she was too smart for that, having been party to that sort of activity before. He set the rest of the grapes down and burrowed down under the covers. He lay down on his side, facing her. "Lyddie, you really must spare—"

"Spare?" She shook her head at him, lying down on her side to face him as well. "You realize what you should have paid me for the pleasure of bedding me?"

"Ah, but it is not that way between us. It never has

been," Wickham said.

"No, it has not been," said Lydia. "Not since you told me that you weren't marrying me after all, even though you had promised." She pulled an arm out of the covers and shoved him.

"Ouch," he said. "That was years ago!"

"Yes, and you were a blackguard then and you're still one now."

"I am not." He gave her a wounded look. "Why, what we have together, Lyddie, it's bigger than marriage. It's deeper and truer than—"

"Shut up, Georgie," she said, giggling. "I don't know why I ever forgave you."

"Neither do I," he said, smiling at her. Wickham never meant to hurt people. He never meant to make a mess of things. The truth was, he always had the best of intentions. When he took Lydia's virtue, he had meant to marry her. He had truly believed it would come to pass. But then he began to think about money and obligations and where they would live, and he realized it was a very bad idea, and that he must get out of it one way or the other. So, he'd somehow suckered the colonel to take Lydia off his hands, and that should have been that.

There had been quite a great deal of women in Wickham's past. Some he simply flirted with, and some he managed to wheedle into bed. He rarely paid for the privilege, truthfully. He had been gifted or cursed with a certain charm. People liked him. It seemed a gift, but there were times when he was convinced it was a curse.

Why, for instance, had he caught the favor of old Mr. Darcy all those years ago? Wickham didn't know. He was an engaging child, even back then. Old Mr. Darcy meant to help Wickham, but he only made him miserable. Now, Wickham knew the taste of all the things that he could not have. Wickham wanted to be a gentleman, but he was not. His suffering was increased. Perhaps if he'd never been sent to school, never been coddled by the old man, never had all the opportunities he'd had, he would have been happy with less.

Well, he liked to tell himself so, anyway.

Wickham was also given to fits of self-pity. He tended to inflate his own sorrows far past the amount that he should, making himself seem even sorrier by comparison.

At any rate, his charm led him where it did, and he tended to have his pick of women. Always had. But there was something about Lydia. She was different.

Lydia was a kindred spirit, truly. She was just like him. Charming, sweet, eager to please, happy to drink and dance and be merry. They were two of a kind. He loved her. As much as he could love, anyway, in any given moment. His love was selfish and short-sighted. It did not mean that he would put her first or put her needs above his. But as much as George Wickham could have a soul mate, Lydia was his.

"Besides," Wickham said suddenly, "it would have all been awful if we had married. Think of the rathole we would have had to live in. Now, you are the most sought-after courtesan in London, and I am..." He grimaced. "Well, I am a pitiful sod, but you, my darling, you are magnificent. You have done much better without me."

"That is quite true," said Lydia. "You are an anchor weighing me down. And I can't spare any more money for you. I simply can't. I have told you about my mother's gambling debts and the state of my sisters, have I not?"

"I thought Elizabeth was bedding Chivsworth to take care of all that."

"Oh, no," said Lydia. "Not Chivsworth. Darcy."

Wickham sat up straight. "What? Darcy made her his mistress? Why, I didn't think the stick in the mud had it in him."

"Apparently, he does," said Lydia. "And whatever is the case with Elizabeth, there is still not any extra money left for you."

Wickham chuckled. "Oh, I remember how much that Elizabeth despised Darcy. She hated him with a fiery passion."

"Well, she doesn't anymore," said Lydia.

He turned to her sharply. "No?"

"No."

Wickham grimaced. "It would have been a lot more fun to think that Darcy was paying for a woman who despised him. Ah, well."

* * *

"This... this was a feast you brought us, Lizzy," said Jane.

"Oh, it wasn't much," said Elizabeth. "There was extra from last night's supper at the house where I am serving, and they asked me to take it before it all went bad." Elizabeth and her sister were in the sitting room at the house where the remaining Bennet sisters resided. They were alone now. It was late, and Mary and Kitty had gone to bed. Elizabeth had been about to take her leave, but Jane had asked to stay and talk.

"Yes, so you said." Jane eyed her. "Do you think I am stupid, Lizzy?"

"What? Of course not."

"Then why do you feed me the same stories that you feed the younger girls and think that I will eat them up just as they do? They are happy enough with the meat and the wine and pies, I know. They will believed anything you say as long as it means their bellies are full. But I am more discerning. I am engaged in helping you run the finances of this household. So, I know better."

"I don't know what you are going on about," said Elizabeth.

"Really?" Jane folded her arms over her chest. "Yesterday, I went to make a payment to the Morleys, because we are paying them in increments, as you know."

"Jane, I told you to let me handle—"

"Well, it was all paid up," said Jane. "So, I took the

money to Mr. Pratt instead, and he accepted it, but I asked him the balance, and it had shrunk rather considerably."

Elizabeth looked away.

"You did it, didn't you?" said Jane. "You agreed to be Chivsworth's mistress."

Elizabeth sighed. "Listen, you must understand—"

"Lizzy, how could you? You have thrown it all away. Your good name. Your virtue. Your honor. And for what? For money?"

"To keep us out of prison!" Elizabeth protested. "And I didn't have a good name to begin with."

"Because of that business with Cumberbottom? But that doesn't even compare to this. What you would go through now if you were discovered, what the whole family would go through, is so much worse."

"Well, it would be the same with Lydia," said Elizabeth.

"And how are you bearing it? Is he awful, Chivsworth?"

"Oh," said Elizabeth, "it is not Chivsworth."

"No?"

"You remember when Mr. Darcy came to call?"

Jane's eyes widened like tea cup saucers. "Mr. Darcy has made you his mistress!"

Elizabeth nodded and then folded her hands in her lap.

"Oh, he is as wretched a man as we originally thought, is he not?" said Jane. She laughed suddenly, a harsh sound. "And here I was, going on about his possibly proposing to you. What a thing to think. Of course, he would never lower himself to ask for your hand. Instead, he simply asks you to sully yourself for his pleasure."

"Listen, it's not as bad as all that. He has not..." Elizabeth trailed off, wondering if it mattered that she and Mr. Darcy had not done the deed. She had spent a night wrapped in his arms, after all. In the eyes of everyone in society, that was just as bad.

"He is the most vile man I know," said Jane. "We knew him. We went to the same balls and dined together at the same table. And then, for him to treat you as... as..." She shook her head. "You know, it's all his fault this happened in the first place. If he had never proposed to you, then Lady Catherine would have—"

"It is no one's fault," said Elizabeth. "There are so many 'ifs.' If Papa had not died. If Lydia had not become the colonel's mistress. If Mama had not begun gambling. If, if, if. But things have progressed the way that they have. Here we are, Jane. We cannot change the past now."

"I thought you hated him," said Jane.

"I..." Elizabeth studied her fingernails. "He has wrought some wrong on our family, it is true. But he has suffered greatly. He has lost his wife and his child at the same time, and he is a broken man."

"So, you aim to heal him by descending to the depths of iniquity? You should have said no, Lizzy."

"We needed the money. And it was either him or Chivsworth."

"You should have made Darcy marry you," said Jane.

"What?"

"He obviously wanted to bed you. He should have done it the honorable way."

"Jane, I cannot... We cannot... We have descended so low—"

"He would have done it," said Jane. "I think he would have."

Elizabeth sniffed. "I wouldn't want to be his wife. Think of it, Jane, being forced to entertain the people in his circle? All those awful women who gossiped about me after what happened with Cumberbottom? I couldn't face them all."

"Oh, come now, how bad could it be?"

"You don't remember the things that were said about me?"

Jane sighed. "No, I do. Of course I do."

"All of it was awful," said Elizabeth. "They called me names and they said that I had no morals or that I was simpleminded or... all manner of things. But the worst of it was that I had brought it on myself and that I *deserved* everything that came to me. When I did nothing! When it was Cumberbottom who—"

"Lizzy," Jane soothed. "You don't have to speak of it."

Elizabeth drew in a long breath. "Anyway, I wouldn't be around those women again for any amount of money in the world. I would never marry Mr. Darcy."

Jane was quiet for several moments. Then, she said softly, "Perhaps that's because you hate him."

"No."

"No?"

"I don't hate him," said Elizabeth. "Not anymore."

"Do you love him, then? Is that why you're doing it?"

"No, I don't love him. I never have," said Elizabeth. *No matter what Lydia said.* " No more than you ever loved Bingley."

But to that, Jane had no response.

CHAPTER NINE

Elizabeth arrived at the masquerade ball alone, because Darcy wished it that way. He did not want to give the appearance of his having brought her to the ball. He thought people might ask too many questions that way, and she thought it was likely he was right. He gave her use of a carriage, though, and she arrived on her own, unchaperoned, in Lydia's red dress with a feathered mask on her face. She felt a little like Cendrillon, arriving at the ball after she had been transformed by her fairy godmother. Elizabeth felt as if she was someone else. She liked it.

She had not admitted to herself how much she had missed this—the music, the spectacle, the people, the fancy dresses, the dancing—everything that went along with attending a ball. She had told herself she didn't care for it a jot, but it was rather lovely to be arriving here, looking out at the room where everyone was standing in their costumes and fancy dress.

The vast room was decorated with flowers and there were lights everywhere—in the corners on tripods and on every mantle. The air was full of laughter and music and an air of excitement and possibility. Anything might happen tonight, or so she felt. A rush of giddiness went through her.

For the moment, she was alone, even though she was amongst many. Everyone was too concerned with the other members of their own party or in looking for someone specific to notice her, so she was able to observe on her own. A woman on her own at a ball such as this could only be a woman of ill repute—as she was, she thought with a bit of amusement—or a widow, perhaps. Maybe even a spinster, although older unmarried women were usually attached to younger ones. If someone was looking at her, they would be speculating about her position.

But she didn't think she had been noticed at all, not even in this spectacular dress of Lydia's. She might as well have been invisible.

And then she wondered if her disguise would be so good as to fool Mr. Darcy. She could get close to him and listen to what he was saying without his knowing she was nearby.

Except that made her think of the first night she had met him, and the thought of that filled her with distaste. It was odd, she pondered, that he could have said she was not handsome enough to tempt him back then, and then changed to saying she was the most beautiful creature he had ever seen. She would have thought the latter simply a form of flattery meant to ease his having his way with her if it weren't for the fact that he still seemed reluctant to actually have his way with her. He truly had no reason for saying such a thing.

So, he must mean it.

A flutter of happiness went through her.

"Miss Bennet," said a deep voice from behind her.

She whirled. There was Mr. Darcy, with Georgiana in tow. She was quite tall and stood only a few inches shorter than Mr. Darcy himself. She seemed to be all arms and legs, like a fawn. She was dressed as a fox, and had a dress trimmed with fur and a very detailed mask with a fox's snout jutting out where her nose should be. The effect was rather strange, Elizabeth thought.

Certainly, there were different levels of detail that people tended to put into a costume for a masquerade. Some people went to great lengths, while others wore a regular ball gown and a matching mask and that was that. But Georgiana's costume did not make her appear to be an appealing young woman. She looked rather strange. If her attempt truly was to find a husband, as her brother had confided in Elizabeth, then something must be done about that mask.

Mr. Darcy was not wearing his own mask. He was dressed in a domino outfit, a large black robe over his clothes and a simple black mask, which he was holding. It was a simple, classic costume, and Mr. Darcy had obviously not put a great deal of effort into it.

"You are late," said Mr. Darcy.

Elizabeth didn't think she was, but she simply smiled. "I apologize, sir."

"This damnable mask is itching my face." Mr. Darcy rubbed at his cheekbone.

"I should like to get closer to the musicians," spoke up Georgiana.

"No, Georgiana, we have spoken about this," said Mr. Darcy. "You are here to dance."

"Perhaps Miss Darcy would care to remove her mask as well?" said Elizabeth.

"No, no, I am very proud of this one," said Georgiana, touching it.

"I told her it would give small children a fright," said Darcy. "It's the teeth."

"It looks like a real fox," Georgiana insisted. "Everyone else is always wearing costumes that don't actually resemble whatever it is that they are purporting to be, but my costume is authentic."

Elizabeth cleared her throat. "I, um, I don't know that authenticity is quite the point of a masked ball."

"No?" said Georgiana, sounding a bit worried. "Is it not?" Then she cocked her head. "I say, Fitzwilliam, you have not introduced us."

"Oh," said Darcy, who was stretching his mask back over his head. "Yes, well, um, this is my sister Miss Darcy. And Miss Darcy, this is Mrs. Fieldstone."

They had agreed that she should not go by her name, but by a made-up persona. Darcy thought it was easier if she were the widow of some businessman who'd made his fortune in trade. She couldn't pretend to be part of any of the older, well-respected families. Everyone knew everyone that way. This way, she could seem to have appeared out of nowhere. Her late husband had been from America, they had decided.

"A pleasure to meet you," said Georgiana.

"No, the pleasure is all mine," said Elizabeth.

"Now, as you were saying?" said Georgiana.

"Excuse me?" Elizabeth had quite forgotten that she was saying anything at all.

"You said that the point of a ball was not authenticity. What is it?"

"I think... it is rather more important to appear..." Oh dear, what could she say that would not offend? "Authenticity must be trumped by how appealing the effect is," she decided on.

"Yes, exactly, Georgiana," said Mr. Darcy, looking her over. "I have told you this before. You look a fright."

"Now, I would not put it thus," said Elizabeth, cringing.

Georgiana's face had fallen. "A fright? Truly?"

"No, no, he did not mean to say such a thing." Elizabeth glared at Darcy.

"Didn't I?" said Darcy. "I have brought you here to find a husband, Georgiana, and no one wants to marry *teeth*."

Beneath her mask, Georgiana's lower lip trembled. "Well, I did not know. It seemed only natural to me that one would want to make a costume as believable as possible. And I don't even want to get married. I should like to go home now."

"No," said Darcy. "We've just arrived. You must dance with someone."

"You have just said that no one will wish to dance with me in this mask," said Georgiana.

"Well, remove it," said Darcy.

"No," said Georgiana. "No, I like having the mask."

"Perhaps you could wear your brother's mask," said Elizabeth. "He does not seem to wish to wear it."

"Ah," said Darcy, sounding relieved. "An excellent solution." He yanked his mask off and handed it to Georgiana.

Georgiana sniffed, but she took off her fox mask and put on the plain black mask. The effect was rather astonishing. Now, without the mask, Georgiana appeared tall and willowy and beautiful. She was easily one of the most lovely women in the room.

Elizabeth smiled. She expected that Georgiana would soon be flooded with men asking for a dance with her, and she was right. Georgiana's dance card was soon full.

At the same time, another woman—this one dressed in men's clothing, in very tight breeches and an open shirt and jacket which showed off her overflowing bosom—was speaking to Mr. Darcy. "Oh, it is so lovely to see you, Darcy. We have been waiting for you to come out of mourning. Practically every single girl in the whole of London has." She giggled, and it was obvious she'd had quite a few drinks already that night.

Darcy stiffened at this, his nostrils flaring.

The woman took no notice of this. "Now, I don't mean to be forward, but I have a space on my dance card, if you are interested. I have no one to dance the cotillion with, and if should like to ask me—"

"I'm afraid I have already asked Mrs. Fieldstone to dance that dance with me," said Mr. Darcy, taking Elizabeth by the arm and pulling her closer to him.

"Oh," said the woman, straightening up and looking at Elizabeth. "I don't believe Mrs. Fieldstone and I are acquainted."

"What a shame," said Darcy, ignoring the clear hint for an introduction. He tugged on Elizabeth's arm. "Come, Mrs.

Fieldstone, we are meant to be dancing even now." He yanked her out onto the dance floor with him.

Elizabeth was not sure how to deal with that exchange. She had found herself not at all pleased with the way that the other woman had spoken to Darcy, not pleased at all. She realized that she felt possessive of him as well. He didn't want her with Chivsworth and she didn't want him with other women. But he could demand fidelity of her, while she could never demand the same of him.

But she did not speak of that. Instead, she said, "Mr. Darcy, if you do not introduce me to anyone, then I shall have no one to speak to."

"You aren't here to socialize," said Darcy. "You're here to keep those vultures off me."

"Vultures?" she said. "That's what you are calling the single women of London?"

"Picking at scraps off the dead," said Darcy. "I think it's an apt comparison."

"You are not dead, sir."

"No, I suppose not," he said. "But I wish I was."

"What?" She was horrified.

However, at that moment in the dance, they were obliged to switch partners and she ended up in the arms of another man, who whirled her around for several moments before returning her to Mr. Darcy.

"What a thing to say!" she admonished him. "You can't wish you were dead."

"I should rather be dead than be at this ball," said Darcy. "I hate everything about these wretched things. The crowds, the loud music, the way people tend to get drunk on punch. It's all abominable."

"Ah," she said. "I see. Yes, you are set upon, sir. The miseries that you must endure are myriad."

Darcy arched an eyebrow at her. "If I didn't know better, I would say that you were making fun of me."

She smiled. "Making fun, sir? Why, what a thing to say."

And then she was handed off to another partner. All the while she was away from Darcy, she found herself smiling, and thinking of their dance together at the Netherfield Ball all those years ago, when she had tried to coax something that resembled a conversation from him. He was a bit of a grumpy man, was he not?

They rejoined.

Darcy continued to plead his case. "You may not think it is so horrid, madam. You are a bright and witty beautiful woman, who enjoys all this noise, I rather imagine. But for someone like me, it is torment."

Beautiful, he had said. He had said it again. She could not stop smiling. "So, now you are in torment? Why, a beautiful woman like myself might become offended if all a man does is complain when he dances with her."

"I am not complaining about you." Darcy was annoyed. "Often, it is quite frustrating to talk to you, do you know that? I once told you that you willfully misunderstood me, and I think—"

"Oh, relax, Mr. Darcy," she laughed. "I am only teasing."

"You *are* making fun of me." His eyes narrowed, but now there was a smile playing at his lips.

"I would not do so, but you make it so terribly easy," she said, and then, as she dissolved into gales of laughter, she switched partners again.

When she was returned to Mr. Darcy's arms, he seemed in better spirits. His voice was deeper as he spoke to her. "I think I am within my rights to order you *not* to make fun of me."

"Oh, you are going to order me around?" She laughed again. "How remarkably out of character, sir."

"I do not order people around usually," he protested.

"Indeed?"

"Miss Be—Mrs. Fieldstone, you are... are..." His gaze was intense.

"Yes?" she said, and she found she had quite been

robbed of her ability to breathe.

And then the song ended, and the dance was over.

He pulled her close, winding her hand around his arm. "I mean it," he told her. "You must stop it."

"I shall be as serious as the grave from here on out, Mr. Darcy."

"Oh, see that you are," he said, mock-imperiously. "As we both know, I am incapable of jesting."

She laughed. "Oh, Mr. Darcy, did you just make a joke? At your own expense no less?"

"Certainly not," he said. "I could never do such a thing. As you say, it would be remarkably out of character."

She tightened her grip on his arm.

"Heavens," he breathed in her ear. "I have missed you."

She turned to him sharply, and they gazed at one another.

But they were interrupted by a loud female voice exclaiming, "Oh, Mr. Darcy, I thought that was you! How marvelous."

There was something familiar about that voice.

Elizabeth looked up, and came face to face with Miss Caroline Bingley.

CHAPTER TEN

Elizabeth wanted to shrink away. She had not thought there would be anyone at this ball who could identify her, as she had not had a wide circle of socialization in the years before she had been ruined. But here was a person from her former life. Miss Bingley would surely recognize her, and then what would Elizabeth do? She tried to remove herself from her spot by Mr. Darcy's side, but he clutched at her hand, keeping her from escaping.

"Hello, Miss Bingley," said Darcy in a dull voice.

"Soon to be Mrs. Heathspar, as I'm sure you've heard," said Caroline, smiling widely. "The wedding is next week, can you believe it? I don't know where the time goes."

" I had not heard, " said Darcy, sounding utterly disinterested. "Congratulations."

Caroline did not seem to notice that Darcy was not engaged. "I am so dreadfully excited. They say that marriage is the most wonderful part of a woman's life, and you know, I believe it, for I have never been so blissfully happy in all my years. I have to say that I cannot imagine being more satisfied with my life."

"How lovely," said Darcy.

"Yes, my fiance is a most wonderful man," said Caroline. "Surely, you know of him?"

"Mr. Heathspar?" said Darcy. "I cannot say that I do."

"Well, the two of you must be introduced," said Caroline. " You have so much in common. You both have country estates, for one thing. And you are both so very tall."

"Ah," said Darcy. "Well, that does sound like a foundation for quite the conversation."

It was all Elizabeth could do not to snicker. Had Darcy always been this way with Caroline? She was beginning to realize that she may have misjudged the man, taking his delivery for dullness when he was in fact making of fun himself at times. Mr. Darcy was quite wittier than she had noticed at first blush.

"Indeed," said Caroline. "You would both get on quite famously." She seemed to notice Elizabeth for the first time. "Oh!"

Elizabeth's heart began to pound against her rib cage. This was it. The moment when Caroline recognized her, and the news got all over London that she was Mr. Darcy's mistress, ruining her name completely once and for all.

Back when she had been at the mercy of the rumors about her and Cumberbottom, Caroline had been amongst the most cruel, writing an awful letter to Jane, at once declaring her condolences for the death of their father and then cutting herself off from Jane's society because of the "influence of your wayward sister." She had been heartless and unfeeling, and it would have all gone easier without any word from her at all.

"I don't believe we've met," said Caroline.

Elizabeth let out a breath she had not realized she'd been holding.

Darcy introduced the two of them, introducing Elizabeth as Mrs. Fieldstone, of course.

"Oh, I have not met your husband either," said Caroline. "Can you point him out to me?"

Elizabeth lowered her head sadly. "Unfortunately, my husband has passed on."

"Oh, how dreadful. I apologize," said Caroline. "I did not mean to bring up such a painful memory."

"That is all right. You did not know," said Elizabeth. "Pray, worry not over it."

"So, your late husband was… a gentleman landowner?"

"Amongst other things," said Elizabeth. "He felt that it was important to have an investment in land and farming. After all, tradition is important. But he was also forward thinking and had investments in the trades as well."

"I see," said Caroline.

Elizabeth would have rather not volunteered so much information, for now she knew it would be spread across the entire ball that she was a rich widow with money to burn, but she couldn't help herself. It was lovely to feel as though she had something to lord over Caroline Bingley. She was on Mr. Darcy's arm, and it wasn't exactly a lie. She did indeed have her own income. She was independent, and it felt good.

"Well, I probably shan't see you for quite a while," said Caroline. "I'll be off on my honeymoon, after all. To the continent. For two months."

"Oh, how lovely," said Elizabeth, smiling coolly. "I also visited the continent on my honeymoon. We traveled all over for nearly six months, in fact. Mr. Fieldstone was fond of saying that life was short and meant to be enjoyed."

"He sounds like a wonderful man," said Caroline. "How sad that he was taken from us too soon."

"Yes," said Elizabeth, smiling inwardly.

"Oh, I must take my leave," said Caroline. "I see my sister beckoning for me."

Elizabeth could see Mrs. Hurst, and she was paying no attention to Caroline whatsoever, but she only nodded and said her goodbyes.

When Caroline was gone, Mr. Darcy arched an eyebrow at her. "Six month honeymoon, hmm?"

Elizabeth flushed, feeling embarrassed. "I'm sorry. I must admit I don't like her. She was dreadful to Jane and then cruel to me in the wake of what happened with Cumberbottom. I know you and she are friends."

"I wouldn't go that far," he said. "I am acquainted with her brother, but I have always found her a bit… shrill."

Elizabeth laughed.

"Anyway, you mustn't concern yourself with the likes of Miss Bingley. Her opinion is worth nothing in London. No one cares a bit for her. She is no one, do you see?"

Elizabeth looked away. "Well, if she is no one, then I am less than no one."

"Don't be ridiculous." He gave her a lopsided smile. "You are the widow of Mr. Fieldstone."

She couldn't help but smile back.

"Oh, dear," Darcy suddenly said.

"What?" said Elizabeth.

"Oh, it's Georgiana." He gestured. "She's sitting down."

They made their way over to where Georgiana was sitting.

"What are you doing?" said Darcy. "Why aren't you dancing?"

"Oh, well that awful Mr. Rattiner asked me to dance," said Georgiana. "I hate dancing with him. I can always smell his breath, and he smells dreadfully of onions. It is distressing. So, I told him no."

Darcy sighed. "You didn't."

"Well, now I can't dance with anyone," said Georgiana. It was considered impolite for a woman to refuse a dance with a partner. She might say, however, that she was exhausted and would not dance at all for the rest of the evening, which was what Georgiana had done. "So, can we go home?"

"Georgiana, I have made myself abundantly clear on a number of occasions—" Darcy began, but he was interrupted by the approach of Mr. Bingley.

Elizabeth gulped. If his sister had not recognized her, perhaps Mr. Bingley would not either. She could not be sure.

"Hello there, Darcy," said Bingley, grinning widely. He nodded at Georgiana. "Miss Darcy."

"Hello, Mr. Bingley," said Georgiana.

"How are you?" said Darcy. "Enjoying this spectacle?"

"Oh, I am looking forward to the day when Caroline's wedding is complete and I do not have to accompany her to these things every night of the week," said Bingley, chuckling.

"You are lucky that she is to be wed."

"Yes, indeed," said Bingley. "Both sisters well taken care of. Now I've got no worries." He turned to Georgiana. "Miss Darcy, would you care to dance?"

"Oh, I'm sorry," said Georgiana. "I've refused Rattiner, so I can no longer dance with anyone."

"Georgiana, that is not at all how one should say such a thing," said Darcy, looking exasperated.

But Bingley only laughed. "Well, I'm sorry to hear that. How positively unfortunate." He turned to Elizabeth. "And who is this, may I ask?"

"Ah, yes," said Darcy and made introductions between the two of them.

After that was done and pleasantries exchanged, Bingley said, "Mrs. Fieldstone, would you care to dance?"

"Oh," said Elizabeth, looking at Mr. Darcy and then back at Mr. Bingley. "Why, certainly. Thank you, that would be lovely."

***

When Elizabeth returned from her dance with Mr. Bingley, who had told her she looked familiar, but did not seem to recognize her either, she found Mr. Darcy sitting with Georgiana and looking sulky.

"I don't want to marry Mr. Bingley!" Georgiana was saying. "I don't know why you are always trying to push the two of us together."

"Well, you *know* him," said Darcy. "And I know he would take care of you, and it would all be very tidy."

"I'm not going to marry someone just because you like him," Georgiana protested.

Mr. Darcy looked up to see Elizabeth. "Oh, there you are. Dancing with other men is not part of our arrangement, madam."

"I could not refuse him," said Elizabeth. "It would have been rude. And then I would have been in much the same situation as Miss Darcy, unable to dance, even with you."

"Well, it doesn't matter, because if Georgiana cannot dance, there is no reason for us to stay here. We shall retire. All of us."

And so they left together. Darcy had his carriage deposit her at her house, and he walked her to her door.

"Will you come back?" she said.

"Oh..." He looked a bit flustered.

"That was what we had decided," she said. "Was it not?"

"Was it?"

"I have procured the French letter," she said.

He grimaced. "All right. Yes. I shall... I shall return."

She went inside and made herself ready. After the ball, she felt as though she would like a bath, so she had one drawn, and she luxuriated in the warm water for some time. She thought it might be rather enjoyable if Mr. Darcy came while she was still the bath. She closed her eyes and imagined it, imagined his hands on her bare skin. It made her feel lightheaded and taut in the most pleasant of ways.

But it became clear that he was not going to come, so she got out and dried and dressed in her bed clothes.

She managed to stay awake for a several more hours.

He didn't arrive.

Frustrated and exhausted, she climbed into bed. She was asleep in minutes.

* * *

Darcy felt nervous about bedding Elizabeth. Though she seemed eager for it, it had not eased his concern. Now, he had another worry. What if he could not please her? His experience with women was rather limited, and it had been since Anne that he had taken anyone to bed. That was quite a long time ago now. He knew that many men would have mistresses at the same time as their wives, but he had not wanted to engage in such things until his children were older. He thought that family should be his focus at first. So, he had not bedded anyone besides his wife. And after her death, well, he found the entire business distasteful.

Before that, there was only the scattered, drunken experiences of a young man, and he was not at all what he thought of as proficient in the matter.

There was also the fact that whenever he thought about being with Elizabeth in that way—really being with her—he felt a measure of guilt so great that he found it insurmountable. He felt that what he was doing with her was unforgivable, and he could not bring himself to…

Well, it was idiotic. Here he was, paying her ridiculous sums of money and he wasn't even enjoying what he paid for. It Colonel Fitzwilliam knew, he would tell Darcy that he was being a dolt. Darcy knew that he was.

And truly, if it had been anyone else besides Elizabeth Bennet, it might not have been so difficult for him. But he had built the woman up in his imagination, ever since she had refused him.

He wasn't sure why it was that had cemented her in his affections. It ought not have, by all rights. After all, a man like him never expected to be refused in an offer of marriage. He could have nearly any woman he wanted. Perhaps he wasn't as connected as to reach the highest echelons of the peerage, but he was a wealthy, sought-after man. He had never even prepared himself for the idea that his proposal could be refused.

It should have turned him against her and made him despise her. For she had hurt him. Hurt his pride, yes, but also hurt him inside, made him feel unsure of himself and vulnerable.

And yet, this only served to make him want her more. What kind of woman could have such strength and such bravery to spit in his face thus? He could not have her, so he wanted her all the more. The incident with Cumberbottom only served to make her more unattainable. Now, she was a woman with a reputation. He couldn't possibly marry her. She was forbidden to him. This made her nearly irresistible to him.

He thought about her sometimes. Most usually in the dark of night when he was alone. He thought of her skin and her bright eyes and the way that she laughed and the way that she scolded him. He thought of her in a high temper, refusing him, her face flushed as she demanded to know if he thought any consideration would tempt her to accept the man who had been the means of ruining the happiness of her sister. Something about her passion made him weak. His marriage did nothing to quell those thoughts of her. She was with him always.

But now, he had her. And he was forced to see her as a flesh and blood woman, not as the ephemeral pieces of a dream that he had wove in his imagination.

Upon reflection of his behavior, he was suddenly appalled. He had fantasized about Elizabeth, but he had never sought her out. While he was longing for her, she had suffered. Now, he was only hurting her worse, and for his own sinful wants and needs. He was a weak vessel. He didn't deserve Elizabeth.

And yet, here he was, climbing up the steps to her bedchamber in the dead of the night, going to her even though he had tried to stay away.

He hated himself, and he did not want to use her and hurt her and not bring her pleasure in the process, but here he was. It was so late that the house was all abed, even the servants. He had let himself in with his key and now he crept silently through the darkness.

When he reached her bedchamber, it was dark inside.

He moved through the darkness to stand at the foot of the bed.

She was asleep, curled up around a pillow, her hair in a hastily done braid that fell over her cheek. She must have braided it up when she decided he wasn't coming to her.

He could wake her.

But he was glad that she was asleep and that he did not have to struggle with himself over what to do. He wanted her, but he did not want to want her, not like this. This way, they could just sleep again, as they had before. That had been rather nice. Darcy had not shared a bed with another person often during his life. He found the closeness comforting.

He shed much of his clothing and then climbed into the bed in only the bottom layer of clothes. He wrapped his body around Elizabeth's.

She sighed in her sleep and snuggled into his warmth.

He shut his eyes. Holding her thus, he felt peace.

CHAPTER ELEVEN

When Elizabeth awoke the next morning, she noted that Mr. Darcy's jacket and his vest were slung over a chair near the bed. He had come after all! Why hadn't he awoken her? She called for her maid to dress, but Meggy informed her that Mr. Darcy was down at breakfast, and that he was not dressed.

So, Elizabeth only pulled on a sleeping jacket before joining him.

His face lit up when he saw her. "Good morning," he said.

"When did you arrive?" she said.

"Oh, quite late," he said. "Everyone was asleep. I didn't want to wake you."

"But, sir, the entire point of your visit was to..." She trailed off, looking around to see if the servants were nearby and listening in. Sighing, she got up and went to close the door to the dining room.

She went over to the sidebar, where a modest breakfast was set out. She helped herself to some rolls and smoked meat and a glass of chocolate. Then she sat down with Mr. Darcy. "Did something keep you?"

"Hmm?" He was gazing at her, a smile playing on his lips.

She flushed. The way he was looking at her, it was like the penetrating gaze he gave her sometimes, only there wasn't searing heat in it, only gentle warmth, and it was more intimate for that somehow. "Last night," she said, looking away. "Was there something pressing you needed to attend to? Something that made you so late?"

"Not really." He lifted his tea cup and took a sip.

"Oh," she said.

"Listen," he said. "I think it has become clear to me that I can't fulfill certain, mmm, parameters of our arrangement. I would prefer that we agree that you and I will not engage in… congress, and then never speak of it again."

She sat back in her chair and surveyed him. "I have done something that displeases you."

"No, it is not that. It is only that I cannot get past the guilt of it. I find it insurmountable."

"Guilt over what?"

"Over ruining you."

"But I am already ruined, sir."

"No, you are not. Unless…" He sat up straight, suddenly. "You have not misrepresented yourself as untouched?"

"Of course, I have not been with a man in that way, sir." She picked up a roll and ripped it open. "I only mean that I was compromised by Cumberbottom and that you and I have spent the night in each other's company, even if we have not engaged in anything further, and that is enough to ruin a woman rather thoroughly. So, there is no point in feeling further guilt, because the damage is done."

"It is not about what people think, madam."

"What is it about then?"

"Well, it's difficult to explain, but it would be… wrong to have you in that way. It would sully you, and I can't allow myself to do that."

She sighed. "But Mr. Darcy, I thought we had already—"

"I know that you are unwilling to receive payment when you are not performing services," he said, stabbing some meat on his plate with a fork. "So, I have thought of that. I have need of your help. You were remarkable last night at the ball. You got my sister out of that dreadful mask, and she actually danced a bit. I have been utterly useless with her. So, I propose that you accompany us to balls for the rest of the season, and you work with my sister until she finds a husband."

"To balls? Masquerade balls?"

"Well, any of them, truthfully," he said.

"But I shall be recognized." She had not worried over this before, but the sight of the Bingleys had shaken her.

"You won't," he said. "No one in London knows you."

"What about the Bingleys?"

"Well, Miss Bingley is to be married and will be on her honeymoon and Mr. Bingley will be guided by me if he recognizes you. There is no one else."

"What of Mr. and Mrs. Hurst? They would surely recognize me!"

"If we see them, we shall stay clear of them."

"But what if that's not enough?"

"You will be introduced as someone else, and the resemblance can be explained away if anyone picks up on it. I have thought on this, and I do not think it an impediment to my plan. I need help finding a husband for my sister."

"What makes you think I'd be any good at that? I have never found a husband for anyone. None of my sisters are married either. I know nothing of the entire enterprise."

"Well, you are quite good at dancing and being winsome, and Georgiana could learn from your example."

"Oh, I don't know, Mr. Darcy. It is all so very strange." She sighed. "But I do suppose that I had thought I might have to accompany you into society when I agreed to be your mistress."

"Exactly," he said. "So, then, all is essentially the same. Except there is to be no more talk of French letters or any of those other things."

"I see," she said.

"I may come sometimes," he said. "To sleep. I like to be close to you. But nothing more than that."

"And you promise me that there is nothing that I am

doing that displeases you?"

"I swear it, Miss Bennet. You are quite perfect. It is your perfection that makes it impossible for me to…"

"Sully me, yes." She laughed softly under her breath. And then she shrugged. "Well, it is your money, Mr. Darcy. You are paying me, and I am yours to do with as you wish."

"Oh, don't *say* things like that." He grimaced. "That is exactly what turns my stomach."

* * *

Darcy shut the door to the sitting room in his home. "I really must speak to the servants here about allowing you access, Mr. Wickham."

Wickham turned to look at him from where he was standing at the fire. "Good to see you again, Darcy."

"I'm not going to give you any more money," said Darcy. "You were just recently here, and I am not inclined to—"

"I understand that you have Miss Elizabeth Bennet as your mistress," said Wickham. "And what's more, you're passing her off as some rich widow named Mrs. Fieldstone."

Darcy massaged the bridge of his nose. He was getting a headache. Right behind his temples. "Have you come to ridicule me, Wickham? Do it, and be on your way, then."

"I assume that, since you are not giving out her name, you wish her identity to remain secret," said Wickham. "And I will be sure to keep my mouth shut. But that will cost you."

Darcy groaned. "You are blackmailing me?"

"If word gets out about Miss Elizabeth, it will ruin her entire family's reputation. Oh, and besides, I also know that the youngest sister is the famous Miss Lydia Swan, and I could begin flapping my lips about that as well. If you care about Miss Elizabeth, you'll pay me what I ask for."

Darcy looked at Wickham in disgust. "You are foul, do you know that?"

"Well, not all of us were born to wealth and comfort, Darcy. Some of us must make our way in the world with rather a bit more hindrances."

"Hindrances? You have been given more advantages than most. An education. The chance at a living that would have made you a gentleman. Numerous handouts from me. You are not in any way hindranced, Mr. Wickham, except perhaps by your own base nature."

Wickham shrugged. "Are you going to lecture me or pay me? The longer you lecture, the longer I'll stay."

"Oh, Lord," said Darcy. "Yes, fine. How much do you want, wretch?"

* * *

"Now, this dress," said Mr. Darcy as he and Elizabeth moved together on the dance floor at a ball at the home of the Chadwicks. "Is this one new?"

"Indeed," said Elizabeth. "How kind of you to notice."

"Well, one notices such things when one is being sent the bills," said Darcy, winking at her.

She laughed, throwing her head back, happy in a way that she couldn't quite explain. There was something carefree about these balls. She could get used to this sort of life, staying up late, being merry, buying new dresses. "Well, I had worn every single dress that I owned within the last week."

"And I suppose it would not do to be seen in a dress one had already worn."

"Why, of course not," she said, lifting her chin. "Mrs. Fieldstone wouldn't be caught dead doing such at thing."

He chuckled, and he pulled her close, his hand at her waist, looking down into her eyes.

She felt her heart pick up speed. Sometimes, when they were dancing, she felt so close to him that she thought that whatever it was that made things awkward and strange between them must melt away by the force of the warmth between them.

In those moments, everything seemed so perfect. In those moments, she wasn't sure that she didn't love him, even though she had protested so much to the contrary. But the moments never lasted forever.

And just then, the music ended, and they returned together to the side of the room.

"Where is Georgiana?" said Darcy, looking around the room.

"She is there," said Elizabeth, nodding. "She has a full dance card tonight."

"As she has every night," said Darcy. "You are a miracle worker with her."

"Oh, I don't know about that," said Elizabeth, who did not think that she was making any progress at all. Though men lined up to dance with Georgiana, they did not come to call on her, at least they had not so far. That was what her inquiries to Mr. Darcy had told her. And there were no offers, even though Georgiana was beautiful and an heiress besides.

It should have been different, Elizabeth knew it. But there was something about Georgiana. One didn't notice it at first, but the more one conversed with her, the more one began to realize that there was something a little off about her. She was, of course, not much of a conversationalist, but that shouldn't matter overmuch. Men did enjoy lively conversation with women, but they also did not require it.

When Georgiana did speak, when you spoke with her at length, you began to realize that she was not much interested in anything besides, well, herself and her piano playing. It wasn't a vain affection, not as if she was a selfish, spoiled girl, although Elizabeth remembered Wickham characterizing her as such, and she could see why someone might think it if they only gave it a short consideration.

But Elizabeth could see it was not done out of malice. It was as if Georgiana was missing something. She was quite intelligent and quite accomplished, but the part of her that would be social, it wasn't there. She was unable to interact with others, not in a normal fashion.

Elizabeth did not hold out a great deal of hope for Georgiana, but she did not know how to say this to Darcy.

"I do know," said Darcy. "She has been doing so much better. I think she will soon be married."

Elizabeth pressed her lips together.

Darcy looked around the room. "Well, I am quite happy for Georgiana to dance and to sit here on the sidelines instead."

"You do not wish to dance again?" she said.

"Does that displease you?" He smiled at her. "I would dance if you wish it."

"We are scandalous, sir. You dance with me so many times people think we must be engaged, and we are setting tongues wagging. So, perhaps it is better if we do sit this out."

"Marvelous," he said. "Would you like some punch? I shall procure us some."

"Thank you, sir," she said.

All smiles, he left her there.

When he returned with the punch, she accepted it and took a sip.

She looked him over. "You seem to enjoy dancing, at least when we are dancing together."

"Oh, indeed. I very much enjoy dancing with you." He picked up her hand and kissed it, winking at her.

Her smile widened. She had grown used to the way they were with each other, and it was pleasing. There was no more talk of the two of them being intimate, but she did sometimes wake to find his warm flesh wrapped around her in her bed, and she loved that closeness on those occasions. Sometimes, though, it did make her burn for something more, but she did not ask for that. This was a pleasant existence, all told. She was happy. "But then, if you enjoy dancing, why was it so necessary to have me with you at these balls? Why do you need to pay me to be your dance partner?"

"Oh, I have told you, I don't like dancing with strangers."

"But why not?" she said.

"It is..." He looked out at the couples twirling on the dance floor. "The risk of it, I suppose."

"What's risky about dancing?"

"Well, it's never about that, is it?" he said. "It's always about some possible promise that something will happen in the future. The women who dance with me, they all want something from me."

"Dancing with someone doesn't promise marriage," she said.

"No," he said. "But it doesn't deny it either. And I can't possibly marry all the women I dance with. So, it's just about crushing women's hopes, one after the other. And I dislike that."

"Oh, you are taking a very dim view of it," she said.

"And say it does go well," he said. "Say that I find someone I like, and that we do go on to be married. Then it all ends in blood and ruin anyway."

She furrowed her brow and made her voice soft. "Mr. Darcy, many women deliver babies with no problems at all."

"But it is a risk," he said. "And the risk is the most dire of circumstances. When I dance with a woman, there is a risk that down the road, I shall kill her."

CHAPTER TWELVE

"I say, Darcy," said Mr. Bingley, pulling him aside.

Mr. Darcy was on his way to get more punch, this time for Georgiana, who said that she was tired of dancing and was only being convinced to continue by Elizabeth's idea that she have a bit more to drink, in order to fortify her.

"Bingley," said Darcy. "I had no idea you were here." He had not seen Bingley as of late, and they had been to a great many balls lately.

"Yes, well, here I am," said Bingley. "If I could just speak to you—"

"Perhaps in a moment? I am in a bit of a hurry, you see. I must find some punch for my sister."

"Well, actually, I should like to—"

"I will find you later, I swear it." Darcy started to pull way.

"Mrs. Fieldstone?" called Bingley, rather loudly.

Darcy's heart sank. Ah, yes, he had quite forgotten that Bingley would recognize Elizabeth. He stopped and turned back to his friend. "Yes?"

"She is Miss Elizabeth Bennet," said Bingley. "Is she not?"

Darcy sighed.

"I don't understand. Did Miss Elizabeth somehow marry this Fieldstone within the past few years? I had thought that after that dreadful incident at Rosings, that she was on the shelf."

"Listen," said Darcy. "I would beg that you not tell

anyone you have recognized her. The truth is, there is no Mr. Fieldstone, and there never was. It is only a story I concocted to help protect the reputation of her sisters. You see, Miss Bennet is my mistress."

Bingley's lips parted in shock. "Your mistress?"

Darcy nodded.

"You... you cad!" said Bingley. "How could you do such a thing to woman of her station?"

"Well," Darcy found himself sputtering, "she was already of a compromised reputation—"

"Which was rather your fault," said Bingley.

Darcy rubbed his chin. "Yes, well, I... it all happened in a rather strange way. But I am helping her and helping her sisters."

"Oh, her sisters," said Mr. Bingley. "What about the eldest Miss Bennet? What has become of her?"

"She is well," said Mr. Darcy. "I am seeing to them all, I tell you. It is difficult, because Miss Elizabeth does not wish them to know about her, er, status, so I have not been able to convince her to move them out of that dreadful place where they are living—"

"Dreadful?" said Bingley. "Lord, Darcy, what is the matter with you?"

"Mr. Bingley—"

"No, I'm sorry," said Mr. Bingley, sighing. "It is not you I am cross with, truly. It is myself. What is the matter with *me*? Why did I never think to look for Miss Bennet?"

"Well," said Darcy, grimacing, "I did tell you that she wasn't interested in you, didn't I? And I recall now that I concealed from you that she had come to London to see you, which would have indicated that she was actually interested and—"

"You did *what*?"

"I am sorry," said Darcy. "It was all such a long time ago."

"When did she come to London?"

"Er, right on the heels after you quit Netherfield, I believe. She called on your sister, but we decided not to tell you. I realize now it was not my place to interfere in such things. I truly am sorry."

"Oh, this is dreadful," said Bingley. "Quite dreadful. All of it. Why, you..." He gave Darcy a horrified look. "I'm sorry, I must excuse myself. I have to admit that I don't feel as though I can continue to speak with you. I am rather incensed, if you must know."

"I really must apologize again."

"No, don't. I can't bear to listen to you speak." Bingley straightened his jacket and stalked off.

Darcy's shoulders slumped.

And then, suddenly, Bingley turned and walked back to him, his gait stiff.

Darcy straightened. "Mr. Bingley?"

"You said they were staying in a dreadful place?" said Mr. Bingley. "Where, pray tell, might that be?"

* * *

Jane was sitting by the window working on a bit of sewing. She and Elizabeth used to do it together, cleverly patching their garments so that they could continue to wear their dresses even after they had been worn through or ripped.

Now, Elizabeth insisted it wasn't necessary, that there was enough money to buy new clothing for everyone. Jane had seen the accounts. Elizabeth was putting money into them whenever she could. But Jane refused to draw on the money. It was all too much for her.

It had been one thing when it was Lydia. She loved her younger sister dearly, but Lydia had always been bound to fall into some mischief or other, and it was bearable to think of using her money, which they did sparingly, anyway.

There was some money for each of them that they had inherited. Very little, of course, but enough to scrape by. So, they did not need to always depend on Lydia. Anyway, Jane could stand taking Lydia's money. But knowing that Elizabeth had fallen to, it was too much for Jane.

How long would it be until they all teetered over the edge?

Jane knew of Elizabeth's life now, all the dancing and the dresses and the house with servants. It tempted her, a life like that. She knew that it must also tempt Kitty. Even Mary might be swayed towards it if she had no other options. Jane thought of their father, and how it would grieve him to know what his daughters had come to.

Suddenly, she sat up very straight, leaving hold of the sewing in her lap.

That... that could not be. There was no way that Mr. Bingley was walking up the street toward their house. She must be seeing things.

But as the man grew closer, she realized that it was him, after all. He was much the same as he been those years before, although there were perhaps a bit more lines on his face. He was not smiling, the way he had always seemed to be doing in those days. He looked grim.

He came straight to the door and knocked.

Jane felt mortified. They had no servant today, and truly, their maid was usually too busy deep in cleaning or cooking to answer the door. They never got visitors. But how embarrassing to have to answer one's own door. What would Mr. Bingley think of her?

Oh, did it matter? He had never thought well of her, if the opinions of his sisters could be any indication. Jane set down the sewing and went to open the door.

Kitty and Mary were there in the hallway, looking eager.

Jane sucked in a breath, touching her hair. Oh, my, she looked a fright! "Kitty, we have a visitor. Please put on some tea."

"Yes," said Kitty.

"And Mary," said Jane. "Bring out the biscuits leftover from Elizabeth's last visit."

"But we were saving those for Sunday dinner," said Mary.

"We have a guest," said Jane, and then she flung open the door.

Bingley stood in the doorway.

Her heart stopped.

"Miss Bennet," he said, looking at her. And then, suddenly, he did smile, and he looked just as he used to. "Why, you are as lovely as ever. I... oh, I must apologize for letting so many years pass without any word. I am a wretch. You must think quite ill of me."

"Don't be silly, sir," she said, and she could not help but smile too. "Please, come in."

"Oh, yes," said Mr. Bingley, laughing. "Indeed." He stepped over the threshold.

She brought him into their parlor, such as it was. They drank tea and ate biscuits, and he talked to them of the weather and his sister's wedding and her letters from her honeymoon. And then, after a time, he fell silent.

And they did too. What was there to speak of?

"Listen, I... your sister, Miss Elizabeth?" said Bingley.

Jane felt all the blood drain from her face. "Mary, Kitty, if the two of you wouldn't mind—"

"We shan't leave you alone," said Mary. "It wouldn't be proper."

"Miss Mary, I assure you, my behavior toward your sister will be above reproach," said Mr. Bingley. "I am not like my friend Mr. Darcy."

"Out," said Jane to her sisters. "Out now."

They left, looking sullen.

Mr. Bingley cringed. "I take it they do not know about your sister's, er, position."

"They do not," said Jane. "She tried to keep it from me, too, but I was able to guess it. It does grieve me. I had hoped that it would not become public knowledge—"

"Oh, it is not," said Bingley. "I will not say anything.

You can rely on my discretion. I would not do anything to harm you, not for the world, Miss Bennet."

"What a fine sentiment," she said, sighing, thinking to herself wryly that he had hurt her plenty as it was. "But I am pleased to hear that none else know about Lizzy. I suppose it is ridiculous to harbor hope for my other sisters to make a decent sort of marriage someday, but I do not wish their reputations tarnished worse than they are."

"I completely understand," said Bingley. "And you are in dire straits. I see why you must think that you must descend to… to the depths of depravity. But truly, it is Darcy who is most despicable in all of this. How could he do such a thing to your sister?"

"Well, we have sunk rather far, sir."

"Not so far as that," said Bingley. "I had thought Darcy a different sort of man. But then, after the death of his wife, he has changed. I know he would not hear of my forming ties with your family, so I can see why he would not offer for your sister and instead engage in such shameful behavior. He is a proud man. Too proud to lower himself." Bingley shook his head.

"Well… there is Lydia," said Jane. "I think he knew of that, and perhaps that swayed him."

"Lydia?"

"My youngest sister. She is a bit notorious. You may know as Miss Lydia Swan."

"Oh," said Bingley in quite a different voice.

"As you can see, sir, we are all on the road to ruin here."

"No," said Bingley. "No, I won't allow it." He reached out and seized her hand.

She was shocked at his touch. She almost recoiled. But it was nice to touch a man's hand after all these years. She allowed it.

"Miss Bennet, I should have asked years ago, but I didn't. I ask now. Will you marry me?"

Jane could not breathe.

"Miss Bennet?"

She snatched her hand back. "I... I could not."

"No?" He pulled back, surprised. "But why not? I will take you away from all of this. I will help your sisters, including the ones who have ruined their reputation, if they will accept my help. I will—"

"Sir, forgive me, but I do not think of you as a man who is very constant."

"Constant?"

"You seemed to have deep affection before, but then you disappeared, and I never saw you again, and you seemed to lose all interest. And now, here you are, back again, as if nothing has passed between us, and I'm afraid that is not the behavior that makes me think you would be a particularly attentive husband."

"Well, yes, but there are circumstances, Miss Bennet. If I could explain—"

"You are changeable," she said firmly. "Not only that, you don't know what you are taking on. I would be a wife who would do no favors to your social standing even without my fallen sisters' reputations, which is why you did not offer for me in the first place."

"Indeed, that is not the case. It was Mr. Darcy. He told me—"

"And so Mr. Darcy decides who you will and will not marry?"

"No, of course not, but... well, I was young then."

"Your sisters did not want us associated before. Now, they would be destroyed if—"

"Hang my sisters! I don't care about them. I'm here because I care about you. I let you get away, and that was a mistake."

She sighed. "It is flattering to hear you say so. I cannot deny that." She laughed a little. "Oh, Mr. Bingley, you simply cannot do this. You cannot show up on my doorstep and ask me to marry you. It is too fast. I have not seen you in so long."

"Yes, but I loved you once, and I think you loved me."

"It is as you say, we were young. We do not even know each other anymore."

"So, you are saying we should get to know each other?"

She laughed again, a helpless sound with an undercurrent of something almost joyful in it. "Mr. Bingley, how can you be here?" She shook her head.

"I shall call on you again," he said, standing up and bowing to her.

She stood. "Our maid is here on Fridays, Sundays, and Tuesdays."

"I shall keep that in mind." He smiled at her. "I know you think me changeable, madam, but I am not. I am solid and loyal, through and through. I'll show that to you. You'll see."

CHAPTER THIRTEEN

It was another night, and Darcy was arguing with Georgiana about going to yet another ball. He didn't truly want to go either, and he was struggling to convince his sister that it was necessary. The only thing motivating Darcy to go to the ball was to see Elizabeth. He could not help but want to be in her presence. She seemed so exuberant and free when they were dancing. He liked the two of them touching, their bodies moving in time to the music. It made him feel so much goodness that it seemed to spill out of him and overflow. Elizabeth was the best part of his life.

While they used to arrived separately, he had done away with all that lately. He and Elizabeth arrived together, in his coach, and he didn't care what anyone said about it. Everyone was scandalized. They all whispered that he should simply marry Mrs. Fieldstone, because the way the two of them were behaving was improper. Others said it must be Mrs. Fieldstone who halted the nuptials. After all, there were advantages to being a widow. Perhaps she did not wish to give them up.

So, when the footman announced that Elizabeth had arrived, Darcy was not surprised. He had been expecting her. She would be leaving from the house with both him and Georgiana. That is, if he could convince his sister to go to the ball at all.

Angry, he headed down to the sitting room where Elizabeth was waiting for him.

She was lovely in a pale blue dress that was trimmed in a

bit of lace. She looked like a vision, and he got the sudden desire to go to her and begin unpinning her hair, spreading it all out over her shoulders so that he could touch it. He felt hot all over, and then cold.

Why had he signed off all claims to this woman's body again? For the life of him, he couldn't remember anymore.

He crossed the room, gathered her into his arms, and kissed her.

She was surprised, but she recovered and responded, opening her mouth to him.

He swept his tongue against hers, claiming her. She tasted so sweet. She *was* his, he knew that. There must be something about what they were to each other that transcended the awful labels that society had forced upon the two of them. He loved her. He adored her. Certainly, that meant something.

She sighed in his arms.

He felt as if his whole body was alight, even aflame. He wanted to kiss her everywhere. He wanted to pull her dress aside and plant kisses on her shoulders, and on the back of her neck, and...

Gasping, he pulled away from her.

"What was that for?" she panted, gazing at him hungrily.

"I..." He shook his head. "Forgive me. I don't know what came over me."

She took a step toward him.

He held up a hand. "Stop." He laughed a little. "We have a ball to go to."

She smiled. "We don't have to go anywhere, Mr. Darcy."

"Now you sound like Georgiana." He shook his head. "She is being most difficult. Perhaps you could talk some sense into her? Convince her to get ready to go?"

"She is not ready?"

"She is not even dressed," said Darcy, sighing. "She is still in a morning gown. I have to argue with her to get her to dress for dinner these days. She says she doesn't see the point in changing one's clothes for a meal."

Elizabeth shrugged. "I suppose it could seem a little unnecessary from a certain point of view."

"That's the hell of it all," said Darcy. "I find myself unable to provide her with reasons why she must change her clothes, especially since it is only her and me here dining together. It is most frustrating. But you are so good with her. She listens to you. Will you go and speak to her, please?"

"I do not wish to intrude on a family quarrel," said Elizabeth. "I remember that when my sisters would get ideas in their heads, they were often rather emotional, and to have someone from outside try to speak to them might have been far too much for them."

"You are not from outside," said Darcy. "You are like a member of the family to us. Georgiana will not mind. Please."

**

Elizabeth wasn't sure how to take that statement, that she was like a member of the family. It was at once thrilling and also insulting at the same time. If he could elevate her to the status of being a family member, then why did he treat her as though she was less than him?

Well, maybe he didn't. He had not wanted to make her his mistress. He had wanted to make his money a gift. It was her pride that had kept that from happening. Or maybe something else had led her here. Maybe some sort of curiosity, or even lust for him. She didn't know. When she looked back at the steps she had taken to get to this place in her life, she did not know how it had happened, exactly. She could retrace the steps, but it all seemed so unreal.

What was more, she wasn't sure that she would have changed anything. She was as close to happy as she had been in a long time. It had been many long, long years of sadness for her, and now, things seemed to have improved a great deal.

She rapped softly on Georgiana's door. From within, she

heard the strains of the piano playing.

"Go away, Fitzwilliam," called Georgiana from inside, not missing a note on the song she was playing.

"It's, um, Mrs. Fieldstone," Elizabeth said quietly.

The piano stopped abruptly.

"May I come in?" said Elizabeth.

The door opened. There was Georgiana, in a long-sleeved dress of pale yellow. She looked Elizabeth over. "What are you doing here?"

"Well, I am to accompany the two of you to the ball—"

"I am not going," Georgiana said. "I told my brother that."

"He thought that perhaps I might convince you," said Elizabeth. "May I come in?"

"You may," said Georgiana. "But I fear you will not be able to sway my decision to remain at home. I have been attending these wretched balls for my brother's sake for weeks now, but I am done with them, and I will not attend further." She stepped aside, giving Elizabeth room to come inside.

"No further?" said Elizabeth, closing the door. "You do not wish to attend balls at all?"

"I would not mind, I suppose, if I didn't have to dance with all those awful men."

"I see," said Elizabeth. "You dislike dancing."

"No, I don't mind dancing," said Georgiana. "It's very nice, in its way. There are steps, and everyone knows what they are. It's easy to know what to expect. But the conversation while dancing, it's rather impossible to predict. It makes me nervous."

"Ah," said Elizabeth. "Well, it's your chance to get to know a prospective husband, you must think of it that way. If you are nervous, take control, ask the questions, find out what you would like to know about him."

"But Mrs. Fieldstone, I do not wish to get married."

Elizabeth's eyes widened. "No?"

"I should think that you might understand," said Georgiana. "I know what people are saying about you and my brother. I assumed you did not want to get married either."

"Well," said Elizabeth, considering, "the truth is that I don't think I do want to marry. But is different for me."

"Not so very different," said Georgiana. "You are a widow of means, and I am an heiress. We both have money that is our own, and if we marry, that money will be taken from us."

"True," said Elizabeth. "But is that why you do not wish to marry? You are frightened of what might happen to your inheritance? Because I am sure that your brother would see to it that no harm ever came to you, no matter what happened."

"It is part of it," said Georgiana. "I would rather be free than to be tied to some man. My brother is agreeable to my playing, at least most of the time, but I fear a husband might put limits on how long I could spend at the piano. And I am afraid that there would be a great many duties I should have to fulfill as a wife, and I have no interest in doing those things. And finally, I do not want to have children."

"What? But of course you do. All woman want children."

"Not me," said Georgiana. "I have never had any inclination that way. I like children, but I don't want one of my own. It seems like an awful lot of responsibility, and I don't want it. I have told my brother of all this."

"You have?" Elizabeth furrowed her brow. "Oddly, he has not told me any of it."

"I don't see why Fitzwilliam can't let it be," said Georgiana. "It is not as if I would be in any danger if I did not marry. I have enough money to see to myself, even if something were to happen to him. I don't need a husband."

"Well, perhaps not—"

"Furthermore, I do not want a husband," said Georgiana.

"At one point in my life, I was nearly married. I don't know if you have heard of this?"

"Er..." Elizabeth did not know what to say. Georgiana must be speaking of the incident involving Mr. Wickham. It was a shameful secret, and Elizabeth thought it best not to let on that Darcy had told her of it.

"There was a man that always been around when I was growing up. His name was Mr. Wickham," said Georgiana, "and he was always nice to me. He was nice to everybody, really. He smiled a lot and he made everyone laugh, even me, and it's not always easy to make me laugh. And he had this idea that we should get married. I told him I didn't want to, but he said that of course I did, and he somehow got me off to the town of Ramsgate. But luckily, my brother arrived in just the nick of time, and I told him that Mr. Wickham was trying to get me to marry him, even though I didn't want to. Fitzwilliam stopped it all then. He made Wickham go away, and I have not had to deal with him since, which has been quite the relief."

"I see," said Elizabeth softly.

"I am quite happy the way that I am. If I am unable to talk to these men while I am dancing, how will I manage to live under the same roof as one of them? It will be dreadful, having to move in with a stranger. I don't want it. I won't get married. I simply won't."

Elizabeth gave Georgiana a shrewd look. "I think that you know yourself rather well, Miss Darcy."

"Thank you, Mrs. Fieldstone."

"I shall tell your brother you will not be attending the ball tonight."

***

"What do you mean she isn't going?" said Darcy. "Weren't you able to convince her?"

"In truth, I did not really try," said Elizabeth. "She had made her mind up about it, and she seemed very rational about the entire idea. It was wholly unlike my younger sisters' tantrums years ago. Your sister is rather in possession of herself. She knows what she is about."

"She thinks she knows what she wants, but she is being ridiculous," said Darcy.

"Why didn't you tell me that Miss Darcy does not wish to marry?" said Elizabeth.

"Because she is only saying that out of fear. She is very shy, and she only thinks that she does not want to marry. But once she was settled, she would adjust to it all very well, and she would have no problems."

"I don't know about that, Mr. Darcy," she said.

He squared his shoulders. "What are you saying?"

"Well, she has some good points. She doesn't need to marry, because she can take care of herself. She has the means to do so."

"The financial means, but not the capability. She has been very sheltered. She knows nothing of the evils of the world."

"So, you would foist her on some man she hardly knows?"

"No, not foist. I would have her form a bond with a good man," said Darcy. "Someone who will look after her properly. That is a husband's job after all."

"So, you resent being forced to look after your sister, and wish someone else would do the job?"

"No! Goodness, no. Of course not. I adore my sister. Why would you say such a thing?"

"I think that I am just trying to understand," said Elizabeth. "I don't know what it is that is making you want the marriage so much."

"It's what I'm supposed to do. As her brother and guardian, I am to find her a proper husband and ensure she is happily married. It's important."

"Yes, but your sister… well, maybe she is not cut from the right cloth to be a wife."

"Don't say that!"

"Well, she says it herself. She likes to play piano. She likes it more than anything, and it is all she likes. She wants to devote her life to the study of music. She does not have room for a husband or children. She doesn't want the distractions."

"Well, she can't devote herself to music," said Darcy. "Because she is a woman of gentle birth, and she must marry someone and provide him with heirs."

"But why?" said Elizabeth.

"Because that is the way things are done."

She gave him a look.

He sighed. "Because I worry about her. I want her nicely settled, so that if something happened to me, I would know she had someone."

"But Mr. Darcy, could she not stay with you? Or could she not retire to one of your country estates and be there, undisturbed and happy? You could visit when you wished, and she would no longer be miserable."

"Oh, she is not miserable," said Mr. Darcy.

"Listen, I do not mean to say things that are out of turn or not my place," said Elizabeth. "But there is something about your sister. She is... different."

Darcy looked down at his feet.

"I don't know that she thinks about things the same way as the rest of us."

"What does that mean?"

"Just that..." Elizabeth wrung out her hands. "Oh, don't you think it odd that no one has been offering for her hand all this time? She is so wealthy and there should be men lined up to try to marry her. But they don't even offer."

"Well, that's only because..."

"Because she is different," said Elizabeth.

"No, I can't accept that," said Darcy. "She could do just fine for herself. She's only shy. If you would help her, Miss Bennet, I think it would make all the difference."

"Me? What? Why?"

"Because you are lively and witty and a joy to dance with," said Darcy. "She needs you to teach her how to converse with men. Once she can do that, it will all work out."

"I don't think so," said Elizabeth. "I'm sorry, but I don't."

"Well, would you at least try?" said Darcy. "We shall all retire to the country, to one of the estates I own. And then you shall tutor Georgiana in how to find a husband."

"But Mr. Darcy, I do not know how to find a husband."

"Why do you say that?"

"Because I haven't *got* a husband."

He waved that away. "You easily could have had one. You just denied all the proposals you received."

She looked away, feeling stung.

"I didn't mean…" He took her hand. His voice dropped in pitch. "You know, Miss Bennet, if things were different…"

Don't say it, she thought. *Don't say it.*

But he didn't say anything else, and the unfinished sentence simply hung in the air between them.

CHAPTER FOURTEEN

"Well, I don't know how long it will be," said Elizabeth, looking down into her empty tea cup. She was sitting in the parlor with her sister Jane. She had finished her tea a long time ago, in fact. It was late, and her younger sisters were already in bed. She and Jane were up late together, talking. "A few weeks perhaps, or even a month. However long it will take me to convince Mr. Darcy that his sister is hopeless and cannot learn to flirt."

"That is what he wants you to do? To teach her to flirt?" Jane laughed. "You, Lizzy, are hardly a flirt. You have too sharp a tongue in your head. Mr. Darcy ought to employ Kitty instead, although she may be a bit rusty."

Elizabeth couldn't help but flinch.

"Oh, I didn't mean to employ her in that way," said Jane hastily.

"No, I know that," said Elizabeth, shaking it away. "I am sorry. I don't know why it bothered me to hear you say that. It should not have." Mr. Darcy would never do that, in any case. He had not wanted to employ Elizabeth, let alone one of her younger sisters. "And anyway, you are right. I am not the woman for the job. Indeed, I am convinced that Mr. Darcy is forcing something on his sister that she does not desire."

"Oh, but every woman wishes for a husband," said Jane. "Why, if any of us had one—"

"Yes, a husband would be a balm for the family," said Elizabeth. "But that is only because of the fact that we have

117

such financial issues. If that was not a problem, we would not need anything. In fact, if you would only accept the money that I am offering, between my money and Lydia's, we could get on much better, and then we would not need to worry about anyone getting married."

"No, our situation is nothing like Miss Darcy's," said Jane. "I will grant you the fact that she may not be in need of a husband in the same way that one of us might benefit, but our family is in dire need of respectability."

"Oh, Jane, we have no respectability."

Jane laughed a little. "Well, I don't know what to say anyway. I had an offer of marriage myself, and I did not jump on it."

"An offer of marriage? From whom?"

"From Mr. Bingley and recently too."

"What? Why have I been here all afternoon and heard nothing of this? Not even from Kitty? I can't believe she would conceal such a thing."

"I asked Kitty and Mary not to say anything. They only obliged me because I promised that I should do their chores for them on the morrow."

"So, you were not going to tell me?" Elizabeth shook her head.

"I was, in my own time. I have found it so confusing, I must say. He appeared out of nowhere, and he proposed almost straightaway. I did not know what to do."

"I don't understand how Mr. Bingley even knew how to find you."

"I understand that he begged our address from Mr. Darcy. He knows of you and of Lydia now, as well, because I told him. He promised to keep all of that to himself, however."

"And yet he still proposed?"

"He did."

"Why did you not accept him?"

"I…" Jane took a deep breath. "Well, there is the fact that

he disappeared on me all those years ago, and without a word at that. How could I trust him?"

"That is true," said Elizabeth carefully. "He came to find you, though, and was still interested in your hand after all this time, and after all that he knows. That is important."

"Yes, and he has been coming back, calling on me nearly every day. I find myself looking forward to seeing him."

"You do still love him, don't you, Jane?" Elizabeth searched her sister's face, looking for the truth.

Jane looked away, but there was a helpless expression on her face that gave everything away.

"And yet you have not told him that you will marry him?"

"Well, he has not renewed his proposal."

"And if he does?"

"Oh, Lizzy, let me be." Jane gave her an exasperated look, but there was a smile behind it. "I shall not throw everything away for pride. You know me better than that."

* * *

Mr. Darcy's estate in Litwithshire was not as large as Pemberley, although it did have extensive grounds and farmland that paid the Darcy estate as their landlord. Elizabeth had never seen Pemberley, but she was told this by Meggy, who had it from the other servants in the house. Meggy was awed by the surroundings. She had grown up in London and had never been to the country. She had never seen a country estate. It was her first time working as a lady's maid, and that was largely because it was more difficult to find experienced maids willing to work for a man's mistress.

Meggy was a sweet girl, though, and Elizabeth was quite fond of her.

The trip to Litwithshire had taken the entire day. They had left early and not arrived until long after nightfall, in time only to fall into bed. There hadn't been much time to explore the house then, and Elizabeth had been exhausted.

Meggy, on the other hand, was younger and more

curious and gave Elizabeth tales of the place the next morning as she helped Elizabeth dress and put her hair up for breakfast. Unlike her own little house in London, where she and Mr. Darcy could be informal together at breakfast, actual clothing would be required here.

"It's huge, miss," said Meggy, running a brush through Elizabeth's hair. "I've never been inside a house so big. Rooms and rooms and more rooms. And the servants' quarters are enormous. There are so many people who work here, even though no one lives here besides them."

"Well, the estate has to keep running," said Elizabeth. "Because the master of the house could come home at any time."

"Yes," said Meggy. "And the entire staff is in a tizzy, because Mr. Darcy is so particular. The last time he was here, he had his wife with him, and she was pregnant, and everyone did something that didn't please him. He strode about the place yelling at everyone."

That reminded Elizabeth of the Mr. Darcy she'd met all those years ago in Hertfordshire. Formidable and in a bad temper. She wondered if he had changed in the interim, or if he simply was different around people he knew better. Even though he was not nearly as socially inept as his sister, he was not exactly what she might term good with people.

"Everyone is frightened that he will start yelling again. They are all trying to make sure everything is precisely to his liking. Every other servant I've met is nervous and worried. I can't understand it myself. Mr. Darcy is always so relaxed and happy when I see him. I can hardly imagine him yelling."

Elizabeth considered. "Truthfully, I don't know that I can either. I have seen him displeased, but he is not much for raising his voice. His anger is usually quiet. He must had been in bad spirits indeed to yell."

"Well, I suppose that he is relaxed with you because a man is usually relaxed with his mistress. That is what mistresses are for, or so I hear."

"Oh, Meggy, do be careful with that bit of knowledge. You know that Mr. Darcy wishes his sister to be kept from knowing who I truly am."

"Don't worry," said Meggy. "I haven't breathed a word of it. I call you Mrs. Fieldstone to everyone. There is nothing to fear on that score."

"Good," said Elizabeth.

"How long will we be here, miss?"

Elizabeth shook her head. "I really don't know, Meggy." She sighed. "I just don't know."

* * *

No one was at breakfast when Elizabeth arrived in the dining room, but the breakfast spread that had been set out contained a vast assortment of cakes and breads in addition to eggs and ham. It was extensive. She supposed that the staff was trying as hard as possible to please Mr. Darcy.

She ate alone and then, with nothing else to do, went looking around the house. There were two wings that were closed off. Apparently, no one went down them anymore, and they would only be opened up for guests. Elizabeth left them alone, and went to explore the rest of the house. She went up and down the open wing in the house, avoiding the rooms where she knew that Mr. Darcy and Georgiana were staying out of fear that they were still abed. She did not want to disturb them. She peered in on the other grand bedrooms and on two ornate sitting rooms. There was also a small library. She termed it small, because it was about the size of the library in Longbourn. She was pleased to have found it, and thought she might pass the morning away reading, but the moment she stepped inside, she heard the sound of the piano wafting down the hallway.

Ah, that would be Georgiana, then. She must be in the sitting room at the end of the wing. That was where the piano was set up, after all.

Well, Elizabeth's task, as pointless as it might be, was to

teach Georgiana to flirt—well, to converse. Perhaps she ought to attempt to fulfill her task. Besides, she could be wrong about Georgiana. Her brother no doubt knew his sister better than Elizabeth would. If Mr. Darcy thought it only shyness, perhaps he was right. Elizabeth should attempt to draw the girl out of her shell.

Elizabeth left the library and went to find Georgiana.

But repeated attempts to get the girl away from the piano were not successful. Georgiana would not be moved from her spot. She informed Elizabeth that she always spent the morning playing, and that she didn't think she could bear a change in her schedule, especially since it had been disrupted by travel the day before. She was already missing the instrument and needed hours to become reacquainted.

Elizabeth suggested that they spend some time together that afternoon, and Georgiana did not outright deny her, so Elizabeth took that as progress.

She started to go back to the library, but then she caught sight of Mr. Darcy going into one of the closed wings.

Elizabeth was seized by the urge to follow him for some reason. She tried to talk herself out of it, to entice herself back to the library and her books, but she found herself darting into the wing after Mr. Darcy anyway.

Inside the closed wing, it was gloomy. The windows at the end of the hallway had the curtains drawn tight against the sun, and there was dust pooling in the corners and gathered atop the portraits on the wall.

All of the doors on the wing were closed except one. Elizabeth assumed that was the one where Mr. Darcy had gone. She tiptoed down the hallway and peered inside the open door.

Mr. Darcy's back was to her. He was staring at the bed, which was only a frame. It did not even contain a mattress. The rest of the furniture in the room had been covered with sheets. Mr. Darcy was bowed over the bed, gripping the foot of it, and his shoulders were shaking.

Elizabeth backed away, out of the room, and she fled down the hallway.

She couldn't be sure, of course, but she had an idea that the room was the one where Anne Darcy had labored to bring her baby into the world, and where she had... had *died*.

Dear Lord, why had Darcy brought them here of all places?

* * *

Later, Elizabeth spoke to Meggy about it, who confirmed that it was so. This was the house where Mrs. Darcy had passed from this world. It was another reason why the servants were so worried about their behavior. Apparently, much of Mr. Darcy's yelling had occurred after the death of his wife, when nothing pleased him at all.

Elizabeth understood it all better now. She could see why that might have affected Mr. Darcy's disposition. But she found this house an odd choice to visit, owing to all the awful memories. She could not understand why Mr. Darcy had thought it would be a good place to get away from the city. Certainly, it was remote, there was that. But it still seemed strange.

Furthermore, she wasn't certain it would be the best place for Georgiana to learn to relax and be social.

Elizabeth did not know if Georgiana had accompanied Mr. and Mrs. Darcy here for the birth of their child. She didn't know if she had been present or not and had all the painful memories that Darcy also had. Even if she had not, she would be aware that this was the place where the event had occurred and it would affect her emotionally.

But she didn't see how she could bring this up to Mr. Darcy. They had already made a significant journey to get here in the first place. It had surely been an expense for him, and it had been a lot of preparation for the servants. There was really nothing to be done about it now, and she had best not say anything. She was resolved to keep her mouth shut about the entire matter. It would not do to bring it up.

After dinner, she and Mr. Darcy found themselves alone in the sitting room, because Georgiana had retired for the night, claiming she would like to be awake very early to begin working on mastering a new piece of music she had brought with her. She had put Elizabeth off that afternoon, and they had spent no time together.

Darcy wasn't pleased with this. He tried to speak to Georgiana about it, but she was already out the door before he could get a word in. Instead, he turned on Elizabeth. "What have you accomplished with her today?"

"Today? Nothing. She wouldn't have anything to do with me," said Elizabeth.

"A whole day wasted then?" said Mr. Darcy.

"Well, I suppose you could look at it that way," said Elizabeth.

"And you aren't even inclined to apologize?" said Mr. Darcy. "Your first day here has been an utter failure. How will my sister ever get married?"

Elizabeth sat up straight. "Excuse me, sir?" A failure? And she wasn't fond of the sharpness in his tone.

He turned to glare into the fire. "Did you not hear me, Miss Bennet?" he said in a low voice. "Or do you simply think that if I repeat myself, I shall say what I said in a different way?"

"I might hope for the latter, because it would give you the opportunity to revise your rudeness."

"Well, I do not believe I have been rude. I believe you have been remiss in your duties. Isn't that why I am paying you, after all?"

She was quiet for a moment, trying to compose herself. "You seem in a frightful mood, sir."

He only snorted.

"Perhaps it is difficult to be back in the place where you lost your wife and child?"

He smiled grimly into the fire. He was sarcastic. "Perhaps."

"I do not understand why you chose this place for my tutoring of Georgiana, to be honest. I would not think it would be the place to inspire her to be more vivacious."

"It's a perfectly good country house," he muttered. "I don't see why it should be abandoned."

"Yes, of course," she said. "But if you are in such a foul temper, sir, I don't think you must feel as though you have to put yourself through the pain of it all."

He rose from his chair. "I think I shall say goodnight, Miss Bennet."

She sighed. She had told herself not to say anything, but she hadn't been able to keep her mouth closed after all. Now, he was likely in a worse temper than he had been before.

***

The next morning, Elizabeth secured a promise from Georgiana that they would go riding that afternoon. She thought that if they were out of the house, there would be no distractions from the piano, and there would be no bad memories of the death of her sister-in-law. Georgiana acquiesced, and they set off in the early afternoon

Darcy appeared at breakfast, but he was brooding and silent, and Elizabeth did not attempt to draw him out. She had to admit that she was more than a little frightened he would snap at her again. She did not much enjoy being the object of his ire.

It was a brisk winter day and there was still a bit of snow on the ground, though the brown spikes of grass were poking through it everywhere. Elizabeth and Georgiana rode through a path in the woods. It wound around the neighboring farms, over a stone bridge, and then came back to the main house.

There had been little chance to speak while riding, as Georgiana had set the pace rather fast, and the wind had been streaming past their ears noisily. When they arrived back, however, Elizabeth insisted they meet in one of the sitting rooms to begin a bit of work on conversation, and

Georgiana reluctantly agreed.

Once they were settled in, Elizabeth tried to begin things in a way that Georgiana would like. "I know that you said that you dislike the uncertainty of conversations, but I think they tend to follow fairly similar patterns, especially when one is first getting to know someone. I thought we could use those patterns to practice speaking to each other. Then you might feel more at ease with the gentlemen you dance with."

Georgiana folded her arms over her chest. "When we spoke earlier, I thought you understood me."

"I do," said Elizabeth. "But your brother does not. And he wants me to try to help you. What would it hurt to practice a few conversations?"

"It is time away from music," said Georgiana.

"Yes, but you cannot play music all the time."

"Of course I can," said Georgiana.

"Well, you could, but don't you find a bit of variety makes things more exciting?"

"No," said Georgiana. "I do not."

Elizabeth sighed.

"I don't see why you feel as though you must do my brother's bidding," said Georgiana. "I thought that was one of the reasons that you wouldn't marry him, because you didn't want to be obligated to him. But here you are, because he asked you to be."

Well, it was a little bit more complicated than that, but Mr. Darcy would hardly wish her to tell his sister about her scandalous position. She did not respond.

"Tell him that you won't do it," said Georgiana. "Tell him I'm hopeless. Tell him to go back to London and leave me here. I should like to stay here. I have not been here since I was a small girl. I have happy memories of the place, even if my brother does not. I have told him all these things myself, but he does not listen to me. To you, however, he seems to listen. Please."

"You will not practice at all?" said Elizabeth.

"No," said Georgiana and quit the room without even saying goodbye or any sort of polite way of excusing herself.

Elizabeth slumped in her chair. This wasn't going well.

CHAPTER FIFTEEN

Elizabeth was sprawled out on her bed with a book. It was late afternoon, and she would have to dress for dinner soon, but she had this time now to relax.

There was a knock on her door.

She sat up in bed, but before she could say anything, the door opened and Mr. Darcy came in.

"Mr. Darcy," she said, scrambling to her feet. "What are you doing in my bedroom? This is most irregular."

"I have the right to enter your bedchamber if I choose," said Darcy peevishly. She noticed that there were dark circles under his eyes. She wondered if he was getting enough rest.

"I suppose so, yes," she said. "What can I do for you?" Dear Lord, perhaps he had decided he wanted to bed her after all. The thought send dark thrills through her—fear and pleasure entwined.

"Why is my sister still playing the piano? Why have you done nothing with her since we arrived?"

"Because she refuses," said Elizabeth. "It is impossible. She will not even practice with me for the sake of novelty. She will do nothing but play that piano. She is very stubborn, and I can't think that she would obey any husband you might find for her. Let it be, Mr. Darcy. Let her have what she wants."

"I shall not," he said. "It is as I said the night before. I am paying you for a service, and I want you to deliver it."

"Well, I cannot," she said. "I cannot force your sister to

do what she will not do. I know not how."

"You must convince her, not force her."

"I don't think that I can." Elizabeth spread her hands.

"Well, what good are you, then?" Darcy's eyes flashed. "Ever since we began this arrangement, everything in my world has gone topsy-turvy, and I still have nothing to show for it. You were meant to help me marry off Georgiana, and you have done nothing to help with that, nothing. I don't know why it is that I keep giving you all that money anyway."

"You can stop!" she suddenly burst out with, even though she didn't mean it. She was relying on that money. She was saving it all up, and soon she would be able to move her sisters into a bigger house... that is, if Jane would accept it. She might not, now that she had Mr. Bingley calling on her every day. And indeed, even before that, Jane wouldn't have been likely to do so.

"Is that how it is?" said Mr. Darcy.

"Yes, let us end this farce between us," she said. "I do not know what it is you even want from me." She drew herself up. "Now, if you please, leave my bedchamber."

Darcy's nostrils flared. He opened his mouth as if he were about to say something, but then he closed it again. He turned on his heel and walked out, slamming the door behind him.

Elizabeth sat down hard on the bed.

What had she just done?

She had severed everything between herself and Mr. Darcy.

But, well, it would have come to that anyway. If Mr. Darcy had decided that he didn't need Georgiana to get married, then he would have had no need for her services anyway. So, it was all the same in the end.

She still had all of the dresses that Mr. Darcy had paid for. She could sell those and perhaps make some money. Maybe a house wasn't necessary, because Mr. Bingley might offer for Jane, and then... Well, would Bingley take them all on? Perhaps he might take Kitty and Mary on, but Elizabeth, with her tarnished name and reputation, she would most definitely not be welcome.

But the sale of the dresses would be something. She could get by on that, and Lydia would help, of course. She had survived without Mr. Darcy for years. She would do it again.

Now, she only needed to concern herself with how she would get back to London. Mr. Darcy would certainly allow her use of his carriage, but she found she didn't want anything from him anymore. She could ride post, and that would be just fine. She didn't need any help from him anymore. She could sever all ties and—

The door opened again.

It was Mr. Darcy. "You have to forgive me," he said.

Her lips parted, but she didn't make any noise.

"I... you are right, I don't know why I came back to this place. It is abominable. I see her everywhere."

"You loved her very much," she said softly.

He looked up at her. "What?"

"You loved your wife, and now the memory of her—"

"No, that is not..." He fiddled with the lapel of his jacket. "That is, I did care about her. Of course I did. But I didn't feel any true strength of emotion, in fact. That is why what happened to her is so monstrous. I did not love her. She did not love me. And she died for it all. For nothing."

"Mr. Darcy—"

"Do not try to talk me out of saying it," he said. "What I feel for you, it's ten times what I ever felt for my wife, and we have never... you are not even..." He sighed. "Dash it all."

Ten times? She could not help but feel her chest tighten, but she did not know what to say.

He kept talking. "But that is not what I came to say. You must forgive me. I am in a frightful mood all the time, I'm afraid. I should not have said any of those things to you. I don't mean any of them. You were right to throw me out of the room. I... I don't know what is wrong with me."

She crossed the room to him and put a hand on his upper arm. It was strange that she felt comfortable with that sort of easy intimacy of touch, but she did, probably because of all those nights spent sleeping next to each other. "It is I who should apologize. Of course being here is difficult for you. I should have realized this and been more understanding, instead of snapping at you."

"Well, I did not make that easy," he said. He patted her hand, looking into her eyes.

She liked the way he looked at her. She realized that it would pain her if they parted. She had grown used to his company.

"Listen, I would talk more of this," he said in a low, rumbling voice. "But not here. Will you come on a walk with me? In the gardens?"

"It is quite cold outside, Mr. Darcy," she said, smiling. "There is still snow on the ground."

"My very eager staff has cleared all the walkways in the gardens," he said. "It would be a shame for their hard work to go to waste."

Her smile widened. "I shall meet you in the gardens in a quarter hour."

"Excellent," he said.

* * *

Elizabeth watched as Mr. Darcy ran his gloved finger through the snow that clung to one of the statues in the garden. She could not make the statue out. It appeared to be a cherub or perhaps some winged chimera.

"It is fear," Mr. Darcy murmured, rubbing the snow away from his fingers. "I am oppressed by it all the time."

"Fear of what?" she said. They were keeping a leisurely pace, both bundled into scarves, jackets, gloves and hats to keep warm.

"Of everything," said Mr. Darcy. "Of what becomes of Georgiana. Of what becomes of the family if I cannot manage to get heirs. Of what damage I am causing to you and your family by putting you in the position I have put you in. I cannot but enter a room without some awful calamity occurring to me."

"That sounds terrifying," said Elizabeth. "Has it always been thus?"

"To some extent, yes," he said, studying his shoes. "I was a careful child. My father used to ridicule me for it. It is one reason I think he may have preferred Wickham—"

"Oh, surely your father did not prefer anyone to his own son."

"Prefer is perhaps the wrong word," said Darcy. "My father loved me, and I know that. Still, I think I disappointed him sometimes, and I think that Wickham's recklessness was something my father wished I had in some degree."

"I'm sorry." She tightened her grip on his arm.

He looked into her eyes again, smiling at her.

She shivered without meaning to.

"Are you cold?" His voice deepened.

"Not badly so," she said softly. "Please continue."

"I don't know what there is else to say," he said.

"You have always been fearful," she said.

"Well, I must admit that it grew worse after what happened to my late wife."

"Because you blame yourself for it, even though I have told you you must stop."

"Whether I blame myself or not, I wish I could have averted it. I fear that there are other tragedies that I could be averting now, but I am making a mess of everything. I worry so deeply for my sister. I am all she has, now that our parents are gone, and I want the best for her."

"I understand that sentiment," said Elizabeth.

"But you think I am worrying for nothing, and that I am forcing something on her that will cause her misery."

"I..."

"It is all right, Miss Bennet. You have communicated this to me already. You can admit it."

"Well, I might not have said it in such words."

"Do you think Georgiana would be happy without a husband? Do you think I should allow her to take that risk?"

"Life *is* risk, Mr. Darcy," she said.

"What do you mean?" he said.

"I learned a long time ago that we do not get what we deserve. Some people are rewarded who do not deserve it. Others are punished, though they have done nothing wrong."

"You are referring to the business with Cumberbottom," he said quietly.

"Not just that," she said. "That was dreadful, but what was worse was losing my father. He was perhaps my favorite person on earth, and I loved him so very, very much. Perhaps he was not perfect, but I did not care. He was important to me. And then he was ripped from me, from all of us, and... and..." Her voice caught, and she could not continue.

"It is true, you have been through many difficult things," said Mr. Darcy. "I had wanted to make things better for you, but I fear that I have only made things worse."

"There you go, fearing again."

"It told you, it is all I do. Feel afraid."

"I could not have prevented the misfortune that befell me, Mr. Darcy," she said. "It happened though I was doing the best that I could not to bring ruin on my head."

"I see that," he said.

"So, that is why it is okay to take risks," she said. "Why I was willing to risk what was left of my reputation to become a man's mistress, either that Chivsworth's or yours. I have nothing to fear any more."

"Because you have nothing to lose?"

"I have many things to lose," she said. "But it is more

important to me to live with what I have left than it is to hide under a blanket for the rest of my life. Bad things will come, but I must do what I can to try to make things better regardless. I cannot live my whole life guarding against possible ill."

Darcy nodded slowly. "Yes, I see what you are saying."

"You do?"

"Indeed."

She waited for him to continue, listening to the distant sound of the wind rustling the snow-covered branches.

He took a deep breath. "Very well, there is no reason to insist upon Georgiana doing something that she hates. I shall risk it. I shall allow her to guide her own sail."

"I think that's a very good idea," said Elizabeth. She looked away. "Of course, you will have no more need of me, then, since I am only employed to help your sister find a husband."

"What?" he said. "No, that's ludicrous. You are…"

"Your mistress?" She raised her eyebrows. "Are you going to change your mind and bed me, Mr. Darcy?"

Darcy cleared his throat. "You know that I cannot do such a thing, not with a clear conscience."

"Then I suppose our business will be concluded," she said softly.

CHAPTER SIXTEEN

Elizabeth could not make Mr. Darcy accept the idea that their arrangement would be severed. She did not truly wish to accept the idea either. But she could see no other way around it. Things could not go on the way that they were. Mr. Darcy would not attend balls if he did not have Georgiana's future to secure. So, she did not see how anything could be formed between them. Would he simply crawl into her bed after she was asleep now and again? Would he keep her in that house for such a purpose?

She thought he might, at least for a while. But then he would likely come less and less, and they would drift apart, and then he would eventually meet some other woman, a respectable woman with whom he could marry and start a life. Elizabeth didn't want to watch all that. It would be easier if there was a break now. It would hurt, but she was sure that if she did not sever the connection, it would all hurt much, much worse in the future.

It was decided that Georgiana would remain behind here at this estate, where she would be happy to continue her music. She would come to visit Mr. Darcy at Pemberley for holidays. Darcy was even going to look into bequeathing this estate to Georgiana, so that she might have even more income than her inheritance. He was not sure if the property was part of the entailment or not, but if it were not, it would be his to do with as he pleased.

They stayed another week with Georgiana, making sure she was settled, and the girl seemed to blossom. Elizabeth had never seen her so happy and relaxed. She didn't even seem to mind carrying on conversations about something other than music, as long as it wasn't for too long, that was. Georgiana spent most of her hours at the piano, and she was quite happy.

Eventually, they went back to London.

Elizabeth resolved that on the carriage ride back, she would end things with Mr. Darcy, a clean break, so that he would understand that there was nothing left between them at all.

But she kept putting it off, knowing that after the conversation, they would have hours of traveling together, and those hours would be dreadfully awkward. She waited and waited, but then, just as they were getting close to London, she seemed to lose her nerve. She could not will her lips to form the words.

Back in her house, alone, she resolved to do it by letter.

She sat down to write, but she couldn't find the words.

After several botched attempts, she decided that she needed some time to think on it, to compose the letter in her mind before she sat down to write. Instead, she began sorting through her belongings, trying to decide what she might keep and what she would sell. She planned to sell the bulk of it all, but she found herself having trouble parting with the dresses.

Each one seemed stitched full of memories. The time that Mr. Darcy had danced a reel with her and he had looked into her eyes with such intensity that she had felt flushed and almost faint. The time that Mr. Darcy had suggested she arrive in the carriage with himself and his sister, as if she was part of the family. The time that Mr. Darcy had *said* that she was part of the family. Oh, and he had kissed her in the dress, and he had touched her shoulder when she was wearing this one.

It was too difficult. She left the dresses lying hanging on the outside of the wardrobe and half-stuffed into her trunk and went back to writing the letter.

It was growing dark outside.

Dinner was soon, and she had Meggy dress her for dinner, even though no one was there except her. It would not do to let propriety slide, she decided.

But then, she didn't seem to have much of an appetite. She picked at her food and pushed it around her plate with her fork.

Finally, frustrated, she retired to bed early. But sleep evaded her, of course, as she imagined a life without Mr. Darcy. She did not want to lose him.

* * *

"What is this?" came a male voice, rousing her from slumber.

Elizabeth sat up straight in bed to see that Mr. Darcy was standing at the end of her bed, looking at the disarray of all her clothing. He was holding a lamp and he wasn't wearing his jacket or vest. His cravat hung untied around his neck. His shirt was unbuttoned. She had seen him thus many times. They always slept together in a state of undress, but the fact she had seen it before didn't mean it didn't still affect her. Her body began to feel warm.

"What is what?" said Elizabeth.

He gestured to her dresses. "Are you packing? Why are these in a trunk?"

"Well, I am not to be living here for much longer," she said. "It is as I told you. The arrangement between us is concluded."

"What?" He marched over and began picking up the dresses and trying to put them back in her wardrobe. "I do not agree. I do not want the arrangement to be concluded."

"I think it best," she said softly. "There is no future in it, sir. We cannot continue this way forever."

"Why not?" Frustrated with the dress, he flung it over her writing desk.

She got out of bed and picked it up, worried it had been

stained by the inkwell. But it was safe. "Please, I may need to sell these—"

"You will not sell any dress that I have paid for," he said. "If you need money, I will give it to you."

"No," she said. "I have told you that I don't want to be given money." Of course, hadn't she also realized that this was only her dreadful pride, and that she needed to set it aside for her own good?

"I don't care," he said. "You will take what I give you, because you are mine, and I am not letting you go."

"Well, someday you will have to marry someone else," said Elizabeth. "I don't know if I could bear that."

"I don't have to do any such thing."

"You must have an heir. You must have someone to pass it all down to."

"Oh, who cares?" He threw up his hands. "Is it worth risking a woman's life for such a thing, for carrying on a name?"

"There's that word again," she said. "Risk. Some things must be risked, sir. It is simply the way of things."

He sighed heavily. "All right, all right. I suppose you're right. I will have to take risks." He crossed the distance between them and grasped both of her hands. "So, then, *you* marry me."

"Marry you?" She tugged her hands away from. She was so stunned, she could only make strange noises with her mouth. Why had he said such a thing? What could possibly possess him to propose?

"Yes," he said. "Don't you see, it's the solution to everything. We can be together. I will not feel as though I am taking advantage of you if I give you the position of being by my side, my wife."

"By be together, you mean..." She looked at the bed behind her.

He snatched up her hands again. "I mean together in every way. I mean that we can share a bed and a home and a future. You are the only woman I've ever wanted. I know it, and you must see that it's true."

"But... you can't marry me. My reputation—"

"Hang your reputation. I don't care."

"It will have a bad effect on you, on your family—"

"What family? You think Georgiana will mind? She doesn't give a fig about anything except what piece she is mastering on the pianoforte. And I don't care. I will take that risk, Miss Bennet. It is a risk worth taking."

Her breath caught in her throat. *Say yes,* said a voice in the back of her head, and it sounded remarkably like the voice she'd used to scold Jane for refusing Mr. Bingley. But, well, she realized now that such a thing was complicated, more complicated than she might wish it to be. And Elizabeth did not want this. When she had admitted to Georgiana that she did not want to get married, she had meant it.

"I know," Mr. Darcy was talking again, "I should not have put on this travesty of taking you as my mistress. I should have had the bravery to ask for your hand the first time that I came to visit you. Forgive me for being such an awful coward, Miss Bennet. *Elizabeth*. Forgive me. I don't deserve it, but I cannot live without you. Marry me."

She put her fingers to her lips. "I..."

He waited, gazing at her earnestly.

She was going to cry. "I don't think I can."

"Of course you can. What do you mean that you—"

"When I think of being your wife, being the mistress of Pemberley and being noticed and written about in the papers and gossiped about for every little thing that I do, from what dress I wear to who I invite to my home, I..."

"Elizabeth, you said that you were not afraid of risks."

"It will be worse," she said, "because I shall be this ruined woman and there is the matter of explaining Mrs. Fieldstone, and ... oh, they will never cease to wag their tongues about me."

"I will protect you. I will help you through it."

"It is one thing to take a risk, it is another to enter into assured destruction," she said. "That period of time of my life, when all those women were talking about me, it was the worst period I can remember."

"But you were also grieving for your father," said Darcy. "And you made it to the other side of it. You are strong, Elizabeth. Together, we can get through anything."

"No," she said, and she shook her head.

"Please."

"No," she said. "But the fact you have asked me, it means so much to me. You can't understand just how much. And I think… I want…" She pressed her body against his, and she sought his lips with her own. She had never initiated a kiss with him, but just now, she felt such a surge of feeling toward him—

He pushed her away. "Stop that."

"Why can't we be together the way that we had planned?" she said. "Why can't you lie with me now? I have never wanted you the way that I want you in this moment."

He took a step back, and he looked stunned and also hurt.

"The arrangement doesn't have to end. Isn't that what you wanted?"

"You would rather be my mistress than my wife?"

She licked her lips. She looked at him, at his broad shoulders and his thick fingers and his trim waist. "Yes," she choked out.

He flinched as if she'd slapped him. He bowed his head. Then he slunk out of the room without another word.

CHAPTER SEVENTEEN

"Are you visiting?" said Jane at the door of their house.

"No, I am back to stay," said Elizabeth.

Jane peered around her. "You haven't brought a trunk with you."

"I will be selling all my possessions," said Elizabeth. "We shall make use of the money. Mama's debts are all settled, and with the money from the sales of the dresses, I shall be able to make things better for us. That is, if you will accept my money."

"I don't know about that," said Jane.

"May I come in?" said Elizabeth.

Jane moved out of the doorway.

Elizabeth stepped inside.

"It is quite a thing to take money that was earned in sin," said Jane.

"If you must know," said Elizabeth, "I am as intact as I was the day I was born."

"What?" said Jane.

"Mr. Darcy refused to bed me," said Elizabeth, stripping off her gloves. She had the feeling of having come home after a long journey. Jane was home, and she was happy to be back in her sister's company. She wanted to sink into a chair by the fire and perhaps even take off her shoes and warm her toes. She wanted to let all the strangeness of her recent past melt away. She was done with it all.

"Oh, well, I knew he couldn't be such a villain as all that," said Jane.

"It hardly matters," said Elizabeth. "I am ruined anyway. It is the appearance of a thing that matters to society, not the truth of it."

"Well, yes, I suppose," said Jane. "Sadly, that is true. But I am glad he did not take advantage of you in that way."

"I am not," said Elizabeth, brushing past Jane to go into the sitting room.

"Oh, no?" Jane tittered as she followed her.

"I don't suppose it will ever happen now," said Elizabeth. "I shall probably die without ever doing it."

"Doing what?" said Mary, who was sitting by the fire with some embroidery.

"Lizzy!" said Kitty, getting to her feet and coming to hug her sister.

Elizabeth embraced her. "Good to see you, Kitty dear."

Kitty pulled back. "If you have come for dinner, you are too late. We have already eaten."

"No, I have not come for dinner," said Elizabeth. "I have come home to stay. My engagement is over now."

"Oh, is it?" Mary eyed her darkly.

"Yes," said Elizabeth. She shot Jane a look. What did Mary know?

Jane only shrugged. "Are you hungry, Lizzy? I do think there is a bit of meat—"

"We are saving that for luncheon tomorrow," said Mary, who had turned back to her embroidery.

"Oh, Mary," said Kitty. "If Lizzy is hungry—"

"I am not," said Elizabeth, "but you are sweet to offer. You are all so very good and considerate sisters. I have missed you." She found a chair and sank down into it.

"You seem tired," said Kitty, sounding disappointed.

"Indeed," said Elizabeth.

"Too tired to tell us all about your engagement and what it was like? Were you in a very grand house?"

Elizabeth laughed, scooting down in her chair. "The grandest," she said. And she began to spin a yarn of her mythic post as a chaperone for a very rich lady and her daughter. But now, the daughter was married. Elizabeth's job was done. She told them of the massive country estate she had visited with Mr. Darcy, only changing the names of the place, but telling them about the beautiful rooms and furniture.

Kitty sighed, enraptured. Jane seemed enchanted by the tale as well. Only Mary was not impressed. She snorted throughout and never looked up from her embroidery.

Eventually, Mary excused herself to bed. She snapped that Kitty must come along or the bed would be abominably cold. "I am not going to warm it for you on my lonesome."

Kitty left, but only after Elizabeth assured her she was on her way to bed soon. She was not lying. Soon, it was her and Jane tucked into bed together in their own room.

They spoke in whispers, lying side by side on their pillows.

"It was dreadful sleeping alone, Lizzy," said Jane. "I am happy you're back."

"I was not fond of an empty bed either," said Elizabeth. Should she tell Jane that Mr. Darcy had shared her bed on several occasions? Or should she keep that memory for herself, to treasure the way he had felt curled around her— his warmth and strength. And his scent. His deeply masculine scent. Oh, she did not want to share that at all. It was hers, her own lovely private series of moments. She would keep them close, take the memories out sometimes when she was sad and turn them over like a worn keepsake. Mr. Darcy had been hers, if only for a short time.

" I have thought on what you said to me about Mr. Bingley."

"Oh, has he been back?"

"Oh, yes, indeed. He calls with some regularity."

"And has he renewed his proposal?"

"No," said Jane. "But I think you are right that he will, and I think I shall accept him. I am only worried that it will be a dreadful union, and that he will always look down on me because of the inferiority of my station in life."

"When I spoke to you of it before, I'm afraid I did not understand."

"And you do now?"

Elizabeth sighed in the darkness. No, she would never tell Jane that she had refused Mr. Darcy's proposal. *Jane would not understand.* Elizabeth wasn't even sure that she understood herself. She only knew that the thought of being Mrs. Darcy filled her with a creeping dread, and that she could not do it.

"Do you think it's worth the risk, Lizzy?" said Jane.

"Oh, Jane," said Elizabeth. "You are the only one who can decide that for yourself."

* * *

Dear Miss Bennet,

I demand to know why you are firing the servants at the house where you reside. They are not your servants to fire, as they are under my employ. You must cease and desist from such a practice. It is most irregular.

Yours sincerely,
Mr. Fitzwilliam Darcy

The letter arrived the next morning, hand delivered by a servant, not through the regular post, because of course it would be scandalous for Mr. Darcy to be writing her letters. Elizabeth told the servant to stay, and she dashed out a reply.

Mr. Darcy,

If you knew enough to have your letter delivered to this address, then you must realize that I, in fact, no longer reside at the house you are referring to. I had thought, since I was the only one to occupy the address, that I might dismiss servants whose services were no longer necessary. But you are right. They are in your employ, and you may see to the matter at your own discretion. Accept my apologies.

Respectfully,

Miss Elizabeth Bennet

The following day, she received another letter.

Dearest Elizabeth,
If you have quit the house that I keep for you, does this mean that you have rescinded the offer you put to me on the last occasion we were in each other's presence? If so, I am rather surprised, as you seemed eager at the time to cement our arrangement in a final and physical manner. It is unlike you to go back on your word.
Tenderly,
Fitzwilliam

She was aghast. When had they gone to using first names? How dare he write about physicality and then give the letter to the servant? Why the boy must be thinking all manner of scandalous things when he looked at her. He might be spreading rumors about her all over London. This was not to be borne.

Mr. Darcy,
You did not seem interested in my offer. And furthermore, I would appreciate your discretion in these matters. Entrusting such words with a servant is not responsible.
Miss Bennet

The reply came only hours later.

Dearest Elizabeth,
You must not worry about Mr. Smith, to whom I have entrusted this letter. He is the most trustworthy of fellows, I assure you. There is nothing that I would not say in front of him. He will not repeat anything, and I daresay he does not even look at the letters. Tell me, has my seal been disturbed when you have opened them? In any case, I did not say that I was not interested in your offer. In fact, I believe that I made no reply whatsoever. I would like to reply now, but I still seem to be in the dark about

whether the offer still stands. Please advise me on your wishes.
Eagerly,
Fitzwilliam

She was livid. So livid that she did not even respond, simply sent Mr. Smith back to Mr. Darcy empty handed. Now, just when she thought she was free of him, he wanted her to be his mistress? He wanted to cement their arrangement "in a final and physical manner"? What had come over the man? And why did she feel like an idiot for not sending him a letter that begged him to have her anywhere and any time he liked?

Truly, she hated Fitzwilliam Darcy, she decided. Why could the man not make up his mind?

* * *

It was Tuesday, and Lydia had come to visit. They were to have dinner later, but for the moment, they were all having some tea in the sitting room and enjoying some conversation.

There was a knock at the door.

Jane stood up to answer the door and then sat back down again. "I had forgotten the maid is here today. Surely, she will answer the door."

"Well," said Lydia. "I did not know you were having visitors. Whoever could it be?"

The maid came to the door. "Mr. Bingley, madam."

"Thank you. Show him in," said Jane.

Lydia raised her eyebrows. "Oh, Mr. Bingley, is it?"

"He comes to visit rather often," said Kitty.

"Why, Jane, you minx," said Lydia. "You didn't say a word to me of this."

"It didn't come up," said Jane.

Mr. Bingley appeared in the doorway.

Everyone stood. Elizabeth moved out of her chair to squeeze onto the couch with Kitty and Mary, so that Mr. Bingley would have somewhere to sit.

Mr. Bingley stopped short at the sight of Lydia.

Lydia lifted her chin. "Well, hello there, Mr. Bingley."

"Miss Swa—er, Miss Lydia," said Mr. Bingley. "Yes, it is good to see you again. It has been quite some time."

"Hasn't it, though," said Lydia.

"Lydia, please," said Jane, shooting a meaningful glance at Kitty and Mary, who did not know about Lydia's profession.

Lydia laughed. "Oh, la, I am happy to see you again, Mr. Bingley. And what a lark you are calling once again on dear Jane. I can hardly believe it."

"Well, my feelings for your sister are rather intense," said Mr. Bingley, looking at Jane. "As a matter of fact, I wonder if Miss Bennet and I might have the room together."

"Alone?" said Lydia, clearly amused. "Why, how shocking."

"Not shocking at all," Elizabeth scolded her sister. She seized Lydia by the arm and dragged her out of the room. Mary and Kitty trailed behind her.

Out of the room, Elizabeth shut the door firmly and ushered them into the dining room, where they all sat down at the table.

"What does this mean?" said Lydia. "How did our dear sister manage such a thing? Is it her beauty or her virtue?" She smirked at Elizabeth. "Perhaps if you were a more principled young woman—"

"Stop it, Lydia," said Elizabeth, glaring at her.

"Yes, it is always virtue that is rewarded, isn't it?" Then Lydia wrinkled up her nose. "Is that a book? I feel as though—"

"Lydia, really," said Elizabeth.

"I'm not being fair, am I?" said Lydia. "After all, he wouldn't lay a hand on you, so it is not a lack of virtue—"

"Not in front of the others," Elizabeth growled.

"Perhaps he likes boys," said Lydia. "I knew a man once that did, but he'd make do with me if I put my hair up and lay face down—"

"Lydia, for the sake of all that's holy!" Elizabeth exploded.

"It's all right," said Mary drearily. "Do you think we have not guessed the depths to which our sisters have sunk?"

"What?" said Elizabeth.

"It's all right, Lizzy, we know," said Kitty. "The walls are rather thin. We could probably hear everything being said between Bingley and Jane if it weren't for Lydia running her mouth."

Lydia scoffed. "I'm speaking, not simply running my mouth."

"You always talked overmuch," said Mary, looking Lydia over with contempt. "I am given to understand that this is all a trial I must face, someone like the trials God gave to Job. I must endure the fallen nature of my sisters and prevail with my own virtuous behavior. I have made peace with it all."

Elizabeth rolled her eyes.

"I understand why you did it," said Kitty. "Both of you. It does seem a better alternative to—"

"No, Kitty, I won't have you going down this path," said Lydia, suddenly serious. "It is not for you."

Kitty spread her hands. "I did not say I had any aspirations toward it myself. I still think I could get married. Not to a grand gentleman, of course, but there are kind men out there, and I would make a good wife. It is only that the family has too much pride to go to dances with common folk, even though we are no longer invited to balls, and I don't see how I'm supposed to meet anyone."

Elizabeth felt guilt blossoming in her chest. If she had agreed to marry Mr. Darcy, would that have meant that Kitty could expect to go to balls again?

But no, of course not. None of them would be invited anywhere if Mr. Darcy lowered himself to her level. Her sister would have to find a husband amongst men that they used to think unacceptable. However, it was perhaps better to put aside their biases and—

Jane burst into the dining room, holding onto Mr. Bingley's hand. They were both smiling from ear to ear.

"Your sister has accepted me," burst out Mr. Bingley. "She is going to be my wife."

CHAPTER EIGHTEEN

"He said that he didn't care about any of it," said Jane. "He says that he has few friends at the balls, anyway. It is a game for younger men who wish to waste their time drinking and gambling. He says he can't do such things anymore. His body is too old for staying up so late and pouring too much drink down his throat. All he wants is a quiet life in the country with the two of us and our children, and he has agreed to take all of you along."

Elizabeth and Jane were in bed together again, that night. Jane was too excited to sleep. She was bursting with plans for the future.

"All of us?" said Elizabeth.

"Yes, including you, Lizzy. I hope you do not mind, but I told him that Mr. Darcy had behaved honorably toward you, and he was much relieved. He said that he had been struggling with the idea that his friend could become such a blackguard overnight."

"Well, it is a bit embarrassing that you told him that. It is none of his affair what I do with Mr. Darcy."

"You're not going to be doing anything with him," said Jane. "You have done nothing with him."

"Simply because there was no... consummation does not mean that nothing happened."

"What?" Jane was horrified. "What do you mean? What did he do to you?"

"Oh, never mind."

"No, you have opened this door. Now you must walk

through it. I shall imagine the worst if you don't."

"He... kissed me."

"Yes, and?"

"And..." She sighed. "He would sometimes come in the middle of the night when I was sleeping and climb into bed with me. We would hold each other all night and then have breakfast together without getting dressed, with my hair down and his whiskers unshaved and ... " Elizabeth suddenly wanted to cry. She sniffed hard instead.

"Oh, Lizzy..."

"I know." Elizabeth pulled the covers tight against her chin. "I *am* ruined. There is no other man who would accept that such liberties had been allowed on my part."

"Well, I suppose that is true, but —"

"I was ruined before, though. Before he ever laid a hand on me. Because that horrid Cumberbottom kissed me against my will. I was never going to make any kind of match. I have no gallant Mr. Bingley waiting in the wings."

"No, you are right. Even if Mr. Darcy has more honor than I had thought, he has still used you rather badly."

Elizabeth clenched her hands into fists to keep her tears at bay. She dug her fingernails into her palms.

"I am sorry, Lizzy. You deserve better."

She needed to say something to defend him, to let Jane know that, in the end, it was she who had denied his offer of marriage. But she couldn't make herself form the words. Instead, she lay there, rigid under the sheets, and kept herself quiet.

* * *

Dear Miss Bennet,

I am running out of excuses to write to you. I could make a letter of sundries and incidentals, tell you of the weather and of what my cook has prepared for my dinner, but I shall spare you this.

I must admit that when you refused my proposal (again), I was angry and hurt and confused. It is not your fault, of course, Miss Bennet. You must realize that I have been raised my whole life with the idea that there are women out there falling over themselves with their rabid desire to become my wife. In fact, the very reason that you caught my interest all those year ago was that you were different than those sorts of women.

Not only because you did not seem interested in me, but because you were so self-assured. Your confidence was a pleasant change of pace. I could not stop myself from being intrigued by you, even beguiled by you. Miss Bennet, you have bewitched me from the very start. I am utterly at your mercy.

I cannot bear the thought of your not being in my life. It was one thing when you were gone before. I had only a brief acquaintance with you on that front. I did not know what it was like to dance with you every night or wake up in your arms. Now, with my sister gone on her own, I am quite alone, and I have time to think.

I have been absolutely stupid. If you do not want to marry me, I shall not ask it of you.

I know not what keeps me from being with you completely. I have hidden behind honor, but I think it is not that. As you say, there is no difference in whether the deed has occurred or not in the eyes of everyone else. Your reputation has been tarnished, and I have done it. There is no honor in that.

I think it can only be the fear that we spoke of, and I wish to jettison all of it from my life. I do not wish to live in terror. I want to come out into the light.

I want you, Miss Bennet.

You have not responded as to whether or not you still wish to be my mistress. If you did not wish it, you would be well within your rights to detach yourself from me. I am not worthy of you. I have never been.

But if you are willing, know that I will not put anymore barriers between the two of us being together. I will be yours, and you will be mine, and that is all that I wish from this life.

If you are willing, meet me at the Birchfield Ball tomorrow. Afterward, we shall retire to your house together, and we can continue in that manner forever as far as I am concerned.

If you do not come, I shall take that as a final denial, and I will trouble you no more.

Fondly,
Mr. Darcy

* * *

Elizabeth read the letter over and over. Each time, she told herself that she would not go to the ball. How could she? She had come home now, to her sisters, and she had relinquished that life.

But things were all different now. Jane and Bingley would be getting married soon. Then they would go off to Bingley's country house. (Not Netherfield. He had quit that place entirely, long ago. Instead, a lovely house in Derbyshire, where there would be room for all of them. The irony of its proximity to Pemberley was not lost on Elizabeth.) They might not be welcome in good society, but they were hopeful it would not matter so much. No one knew of Lydia, of course, and everyone thought that Elizabeth was Mrs. Fieldstone. So, there was only the story of Elizabeth and Cumberbottom from all those years ago, and no one spoke of it anymore. It might be that no one would remember, and that they could all live quite happily.

But Elizabeth did not know if she wanted to go and live in the country as a maiden aunt to her sister's children, to live out her life sedately and quietly. Now, she had tasted the life that she could have with Mr. Darcy here in London. When there was no offer from Mr. Darcy, then that was one thing. But now, this letter had come, and she was unsure of her path forward. She had no idea what to do.

She could have spoken with Jane about it, but she didn't. She didn't know how to explain it without telling Jane that she had refused Mr. Darcy's proposal of marriage, and she could not explain that.

Even to herself, it didn't make any sense. She could not see why she had done such a thing. It was ridiculous. But the thought of being looked at and gossiped over—the awful things they would say, rather likely in print—it would destroy her. She remembered the way she had felt back after the incident at Rosings, and it had been dreadful. It was difficult to fathom the badness of it. Everyone knew this story of her, and they had drawn conclusions about her character. They did not know the truth of it, and they were not interested in finding out the truth of it. They enjoyed their stories better, and they enjoyed ridiculing Elizabeth. They had no thought for her feelings, none at all.

She would not go through that again.

Perhaps it didn't make sense to deny him. It was not a decision of the head, but rather one of the heart.

Being Mr. Darcy's mistress was not ideal. But she didn't live in an ideal world. This was the way that she could be with him, and she missed him. She… why, she loved him. She loved his foibles and his fears. She loved how devoted he was to his sister. She loved the way he looked at her while they were dancing. She loved his smile and his laughter.

Surely, love meant something, didn't it?

If it was love, then being his mistress, it was not so shameful.

It was a decision of the heart, not the head.

So, she told Jane that she would be working on packing things up to sell at her old house, and that she would be spending the night there and not home until the morrow.

Jane was so wrapped up in her future with Mr. Bingley that she paid Elizabeth no mind. She waved the explanation away and asked no questions.

Then Elizabeth went back to her old house, where all the servants that she had been dismissed had been rehired and were waiting for her. She ate dinner, for it had been prepared for her, and then she was helped into a dress by Meggy, who also wove her hair into elegant curls.

When she arrived at the ball, she saw Mr. Darcy standing on the steps outside, waiting for her.

She nearly ran to him, but she could not, not in her dress. Instead, she picked up her skirts and moved as quickly as she could up the steps.

He caught her in his arms, grinning widely. "You came."

"Of course I did." She put her gloved hand against his cheek.

He covered her hand with his own and fixed her with a stare that was so voracious that she shivered all the way down to her toes.

They looked at each other for several long moments before they broke their gaze.

"I suppose we must go in and dance," he murmured in her ear.

"I suppose we must," she said.

Elizabeth knew what would come after the dancing. At the beginning of all of this, she had been frightened, but now she wasn't. She was curious, even eager. Whatever Lydia had said to her, it would not be that way between her and Mr. Darcy. What she felt for him, what he felt for her, it was bigger than anything that Elizabeth had ever known.

Why else would she be here with him, doing this particularly stupid thing?

CHAPTER NINETEEN

Wickham banged on the door of Darcy's house. He was more than a little drunk, and he struggled to keep his balance as he hiccuped. He raised his hand to knock again, but the door was yanked open by one of Darcy's footmen.

"Yes?" said the footman.

"I'm here to see Mr. Darcy," said Wickham.

"I'm sorry, Mr. Darcy is not at home," said the footman.

"Then I'll wait," said Wickham, taking a step forward but misjudging it all somehow and ending up toppling into the door frame. He clutched it, muttering swear words under his breath.

The footman wrinkled his nose at him. "Who are you?"

"I am Mr. Wickham," he said. "I'm a close, personal friend of Mr. Darcy's. We were children together." He was trying to stand up straight, but he was having trouble. Instead, he just leaned against the door. "So, you see, you'll have to let me in."

"Mr. Wickham," said the footman. "No, no, I've heard of you. Botham let you in, and Mr. Darcy was most displeased. He's given us direct orders to turn you away."

"Well, he won't want to do that this time," said Wickham. "Because I've got things that I can tell the world about. All manner of things. And he will want to pay me for my silence."

"Mr. Darcy was insistent that he not deal with you," said the footman. "I heard him talk of it himself. Darcy's turning over a new leaf. He's not living in fear anymore. He's taking risks. And I'm sure he'd be willing to risk not dealing with you."

"Hadn't you better check with him?" said Wickham. "If you do not let me in, then I shall go out and tell everyone that Mrs. Fieldstone he has been parading about with is his mistress, and the sister to the infamous Lydia Swan. Furthermore, they are all Bennet girls, and they do not have the most savory background to begin with."

"Mr. Darcy is not interested in paying you any more money," said the footman. "Tell anyone anything you wish. But get off the steps here and take your drunken self elsewhere!" The footman began to push the door closed.

"Wait!" said Wickham, wedging his foot in the door. "If you don't let me in, Darcy is going to have you dismissed, I guarantee it. He wouldn't want me to flap my lips with this tale. I assure you that when he discovers what you've done—"

"Out!" The footman shoved Wickham out of the doorway and shut the door tight against him.

Wickham gave the closed door and indignant look. "Told his servants not to admit me, did he? Well, Darcy's going to regret that. Oh, yes, he most certainly is. I'll tell this story to whoever I please."

And then he turned and tumbled down the steps, legs over arms, too drunk to stop himself.

* * *

Elizabeth tried to help Darcy's fingers as they worked at her stays. She was laughing, and the laughter seemed to bubble out of her like sparkling wine. She was happy, so very happy, and she felt as if there was nothing in this moment that could change how good it all was.

Darcy was laughing too. "I don't see why they make these bloody things so difficult to get off," he grunted.

"Don't say bloody," said Elizabeth, turning in his arms, putting her lips against his. "We are finally here together, in this perfect moment, and you're cursing."

He kissed her hungrily. "Mmmph, it's been too long that we've waited for this," he murmured against her mouth. "I don't have any patience left."

She wriggled the stays around her torso, still laced, so that the laces were in the front. Now that she could see them, she deftly unlaced them and pulled them off. "*Voila!*"

He chuckled, but then he broke off because he was looking at her, and he didn't seem to be able to get enough of her. He had that penetrating look, the one that seemed to go through her and make her weak, and soon she wasn't laughing either. She was just looking at him as well.

"Well, I am nearly stripped of all my clothing," she said, suddenly breathless. "And you are wearing... all that." She gestured.

Darcy yanked off his cravat and shed his jacket and coat. He untucked his shirt from his trousers and tugged it over his head. His chest was bare in mere seconds.

She sucked in an audible breath. How long had she been waiting to see his bare shoulders? It seemed an eternity. But it had been worth the wait. They were magnificent. They were so broad, and his muscles rippled beneath his skin. She wanted to touch them, and so she did. She put her fingers against his bare skin.

He made a noise in the back of his throat.

She feathered her fingers over him. He was firm—so firm, so wonderfully firm, but yet, the way that his skin slid against her fingertips, it was like velvet, and she shut her eyes and shivered again.

His lips against her eyebrow. "Do I please you?"

She laughed, keeping her eyes closed. " Am I that transparent?"

"No, indeed," he whispered. "In fact, your good opinion is not so easily earned."

She opened her eyes slowly, bending back her neck to look into his eyes. " I thought it was you who had such exacting standards, sir."

"Well, whatever my standards are, you quite exceed them."

"Yes," she said. "And your shoulders are quite possibly the Platonic ideal of shoulders, I should think. I have been waiting so long to see them, to touch them, and now that I have, I am stunned."

He ducked his head, looking bashful. "That's ... preposterous."

"No," she said, her fingers under his chin, turning his face back to hers.

They kissed again.

The kiss went on for a long time, long enough for everything to become nothing but swirling colors and pleasantness, for all thoughts to be wiped out of her head, and for there to be nothing in the world but his lips on hers and her fingers tracing patterns over all the bare skin of his chest and his back, and for time to become meaningless, seconds that stretched out and became hours or hours that turned to minutes, she knew not. Nothing was important except Mr. Darcy and—

Oh!

He gave her gentle shove, and she was suddenly on her back on the bed, and she was laughing again. He crawled onto the bed as well, covering her body with his.

More kissing.

She loved the kissing. She thought the kissing could well go on forever. They had never kissed like this, each kiss going deeper than the next, each making her feel as though she was being turned inside out and that every part of her was sweetness and goodness.

His hand under her chemise, working its way over her thigh, her hip.

She moaned. She couldn't help it. She had not had the knowledge that a touch could feel thus. It seemed to wake up parts of herself she was not sure she had truly become acquainted with before, as if there were secret, new parts of her body that had lain dormant her entire life.

And then his fingers skimmed her waist, and her whole body broke out into puckering goose bumps, and she was overcome with the sensation of it. She gasped against his mouth, and she could not catch her breath, and she began to feel vaguely frightened, as though she might lose all control of herself and become nothing but a slave to this feeling of pleasure. If she had only known it could all be so nice, she would have been twice as strenuous in her insistence that they engage in this activity immediately.

But then this plateau of enjoyment was shattered entirely when Mr. Darcy's hand cupped her breast.

She cried out.

He panted, resting his forehead against hers.

She tried to catch her breath.

But then he was exploring her, teasing her, both his hands on her, and she realized her chemise was somehow bunched up under her armpits and it was most undignified and probably looked very silly, but she didn't care, because she only wanted him to keep touching her. She must have somehow passed that point where she had control of herself and not realized it. She was thoroughly unmoored now, a ship tossed on stormy seas, and everything was bliss.

She wrapped her bare thighs around Darcy's legs, dragging her hands down his bare back.

He went rigid over her, his head back, his eyes slammed shut. Then, relaxing, he looked down on her.

She felt strange, looking at him again. He was here with her on this journey that had unwound her and unmade her, but she was still herself, and she did not—

"Hello," he said, a smile playing on his lips.

She smiled back, relieved. "Hello," she whispered back.

He kissed her again, sweetly, briefly. "Ought we…? That is… the rest of our clothing…?"

"Oh, yes," she said, struggling into a sitting position and fighting with her chemise to get it over her head.

He moved away from her to a sitting position and wriggled out of his trousers and boots.

She had the chemise off, but she was holding it against her skin, covering herself, which was stupid, because he had seen it all already, and touched it too, touched her everywhere, his hands had been all over her skin, and yet she still held it tight. She watched him, watched as he yanked off one boot and then the other and then undid his trousers and pulled them down and then... there he was.

She bit down on her bottom lip and stared.

He looked up at her.

She looked away, shy all of the sudden.

"Is that... have I...?"

"No, no," she said, bringing her gaze back to his. "No, I am ... you are ... " She dropped the idiotic chemise and pressed herself against him and the feeling of his bare skin against hers, *everywhere*, it was an epiphany.

They fell back on the bed and there was more kissing, and more touching, both of them urgently moving their hands over the other, and she could feel that part of him, that male part, the part she found so curious and interesting, pressing against her between her legs.

She wriggled against it, because it was the firmest part of him yet, and everything seemed concentrated there, between her thighs. She should have realized that, since it was all going to end up there, but she had been distracted by how nice it felt everywhere else, how much his hands had driven her mad with sweetness.

He grunted and pulled away.

"What's wrong?" she whispered.

"The, um, the French letter," he muttered.

" Oh, yes, " she said, sitting up. She fumbled in the drawer beside the bed and came out with the container that held it and then handed it to him.

He took it out and turned it this way and that, looking at it as if he didn't understand how it worked.

She licked her lips, wondering if she should offer to assist him. She was fairly sure it was meant to, er, sheath him. But she felt oddly shy at the thought of putting her hands on him there. Was he quite sensitive in that part of his body? Could she hurt him? She knew that men could be badly injured if there was a blow between their legs, and perhaps it was because of the male organ. She should perhaps ask. Or she should have asked Lydia. Why had she not asked anything useful?

But then Mr. Darcy seemed to understand what needed to be done and he did it himself, quickly, efficiently. He gave her a lopsided smile, and his ears turned pink.

It was so endearing that she had to kiss him again, and he kissed her back with vigor and force, and one of his hands was back at her breast, and the other was touching her between her thighs, and she shuddered, crying out at that, at the sweetness of it all, it was so, so good—

Her eyes popped open, because it had happened.

He was... in her, stretching her wide open and they were joined, and it *did* hurt. She whimpered. She coughed.

He let out a labored breath. "Lizzy?" he murmured, worried. "Lizzy are you—?"

She dug her fingers into his shoulders.

"Do you want it to stop?" His voice was a dark rumble in the darkness.

"I..." She didn't know. Already, the shock of it was wearing off, and the pain was lessening. Lydia had said the pain was part of it, that there was no way out of it. It would be pointless to stop, she supposed. "No, don't stop. Keep going." Of course, she didn't really understand what there was to do to keep going. Hadn't they achieved it? He was inside her, all the way inside, as deep as he could get, and there couldn't—

He started to move.

She let out a ragged breath.

He echoed it, and his lips found hers again.

Oh, she thought. *So, this is it*. This was the most intimate thing she had ever experienced. He was so close, all of him pressed up against her, part of his body buried in her own. They were one. They were joined together and they were connected, and she had never felt so much sheer, powerful joy in her life. Tears came her her eyes unbidden and she held onto him for dear life.

His lips on her mouth, on her jaw, on her throat. He groaned softly. "I love you, Elizabeth Bennet."

"I love you too, Fitzwilliam Darcy," she whispered back, and she was floating somewhere. Everything was wonderful.

CHAPTER TWENTY

"Mr. Bingley, you are visiting rather early this morning," said Jane, opening the door wide for him. There was no maid today, and Mr. Bingley had usually not visited on days when they had no help, but she supposed none of that mattered now that they were engaged. He knew how she lived, of course, and he would not be put off by the fact that she and her sisters must serve him.

"Yes, I apologize," said Mr. Bingley, removing his hat as he stepped inside.

"Well, come into the parlor," said Jane, gesturing. "I do not think we have any tea brewing, but I can go into the kitchen and—"

"No, do not trouble yourself," he said. "I did not come here for sustenance." He nodded at the door to the parlor. "After you."

She stepped into the parlor.

Kitty and Mary looked up. They were both darning stockings that morning. There had been a growing pile of stockings with holes in them, and it needed to be seen to.

Mr. Bingley cleared his throat. "Ah, perhaps your sisters might wish to find some other activity for a while."

"Oh, had you not heard?" said Mary sourly. "We have confessed that we both know all the dark secrets of the family."

"Yes," said Kitty. "We have not been ignorant of our sisters' occupations for some time now. So, there is nothing to hide."

"You may speak freely," said Jane, gesturing for him to sit down.

He did so. "I had thought that Mr. Darcy's and your sister's arrangement was over."

"Oh, it is," said Jane. "Why last night, she went to pack up the last of her belongings from the house where he had put her up. She even stayed overnight."

"Oh, did she," said Mr. Bingley darkly.

Jane furrowed her brow. "I suppose it is odd for her to stay overnight. She said there was little she could pack, anyway, only the dresses, and she wanted to arrange for those to be sold, and so…" She looked up. "I think Lizzy lied to us."

"Indeed," said Mr. Bingley. "She and Mr. Darcy were seen together at the Birchfield Ball last night, dancing together. But they didn't stay long. They both disappeared early in the evening. The sight of her—Mrs. Fieldstone—is always enough to get tongues wagging, because they dance far too many dances together, and they arrive and leave together, and never a hint of a marriage proposal, and everyone already thinks that Mrs. Fieldstone is a woman of very loose morals. But the way they were dancing last night…" He shook his head. "They were especially scandalous."

Jane sighed. She rubbed her temples. "I don't know what has got into Lizzy. Mr. Darcy is the very devil. I had thought he was taking the honorable path with her, but he is dragging her down the broad way of destruction again. She loses her head when it comes to him, I'm afraid."

"Yes, it appears so," said Bingley. "Listen, your sister is welcome in our home when we are wed, but not if she is… entertaining gentleman. That goes for all of them. I must draw the line somewhere."

"I agree," said Jane. "It is quite one thing if she has seen the error of her ways and is trying to reform. There is forgiveness for those who ask. But if she does not wish to change, then what can we do?" She stood up. "I shall write to her and tell her that she must choose between Mr. Darcy and her family. She cannot have it both ways. Do you have a servant who could deliver the letter?"

"Of course," said Mr. Bingley. His shoulders slumped. "Are you certain, dearest? I do not wish to cause you pain, and if you wished to try to convince me otherwise—"

"No, sir," said Jane, shaking her head. "It is not you who is causing me pain. You, in fact, are the soul of reason. I am overwhelmed by your generosity."

Mr. Bingley's expression changed to something rather smoldering.

Jane's breath caught in her throat. Oh, dear, she was feeling rather flushed. "Paper," she said in a strained voice. "I need paper and a pen!"

* * *

Elizabeth woke as sunlight streamed in the window, and she was gloriously undressed, wearing nothing at all. She liked the way the sheets felt on her bare skin. She rolled over, sighing softly.

Mr. Darcy moaned next to her, his mouth moving against her shoulder, his fingers crawling slowly up over her hip and walking over her belly button.

She let out a tiny squeal.

He growled and began to kiss his way up her shoulder and neck to find her earlobe.

Pleasure exploded through her body, hot and sweet. She gasped, clinging to him.

His hands were roaming over her, finding her sensitive places. She could feel his body pressing against her. That male part of him was stiffening.

"Are you too sore?" he whispered in her ear.

"I…" She kissed him. "No."

His fingers darted between her legs.

She moaned.

"You want this?"

"Yes," she sighed. "Yes, yes, yes."

And then there was no more talking, none at all, and she *was* sore, but it was a sweet soreness that felt good at the same time, and she thought she would very much like to spend the rest of the day in bed, sleeping and waking to do this over and over again.

But once they were spent, and resting in each other's arms in the bed, holding onto each other, there was a tentative knock at the door.

"Madam?" Meggy's voice was a squeak and the door remained closed, though Meggy usually opened it to speak to Elizabeth.

Darcy tightened his grip on her shoulders. He kissed her temple. "Tell her to go away."

Elizabeth giggled. "Is it important, Meggy?"

"There's a letter from your sister," said Meggy. "The servant who brought it has been instructed to wait for a reply."

Elizabeth furrowed her brow. "My sister?" Oh dear, was it bad news? Had something happened? She shoved aside the covers and climbed out of bed. Oh, the cold morning air was less than welcome on her bare skin. And she couldn't find her clothing. What had happened to her chemise? It wouldn't be enough, but it would at least cover everything.

She remembered throwing it, but where had she thrown it and —

Mr. Darcy pulled it out from beneath his pillow. "Looking for this?"

"Yes, thank you." She took it from him. "Oh, I am sorry for —"

"No, go and read the letter from your sister," he said. "Of course, you must."

She smiled at him and then pulled her chemise over her head. She went to the door and opened it a crack. She did not want Meggy to see Mr. Darcy. That wouldn't do.

But then she couldn't go marching about the house in the

chemise. And Mr. Bingley's servant could not see her only dressed thus.

Luckily, Meggy held out the letter, her eyes averted, her face blood red.

"Thank you, Meggy," said Elizabeth, and now she felt mortified. She had been rather noisy had she not? All of the servants would have heard, and now… She shuddered, and now her own face was heating up.

But there was no time to think on it. She sat down at her desk and opened the letter. She read it quickly once through and then started at the beginning and read it more slowly, now that she had determined no one was ill or in danger or hurt.

After the second read-through, she closed the letter and took out a piece of paper. She wrote a quick response back to Jane that said that she had indeed chosen Mr. Darcy and London, and that she hoped that her family would not shun her, but she would understand if they must. She folded it up.

"What?" said Mr. Darcy, who was now sitting on the bed wearing his trousers but no shirt. "What does the letter say?"

"I had thought I would be able to tell her myself," said Elizabeth. "But I had forgotten of her connection to Mr. Bingley now. Of course, tongues would have been wagging about us at the ball last night. He would have told her of it before I got the chance. She is angry with me."

"Her connection to Mr. Bingley?" Darcy raised his eyebrows.

"Yes, they are to be married." Elizabeth smiled. "I am happy for her. Lord knows Jane deserves this. She is so good. Much better than I shall ever be. I am… well, wicked."

Darcy rubbed his chin, not meeting her gaze. "Married?"

They were quiet.

"I don't know if Bingley will insist that she not associate with me," said Elizabeth. "I have told her that I do not blame her if it must be so."

Darcy sniffed. He got up off the bed and fished his shirt up off the floor. He shrugged into it. "Well, you have made your choices, I suppose."

"Don't be like that," said Elizabeth. "Not after everything was so… so good between us."

"I am not being like anything," said Darcy, tucking in his shirt.

"You are. You are cold to me now, out of nowhere, when a moment ago, I could have sworn you wanted to have me again and that—"

He turned on her, grasping her shoulders, and cutting off her words by crushing his lips against hers.

She went limp against him, surrendering to the kiss, everything falling away. He was the only thing keeping her upright.

And then he let go of her, and she stumbled before righting herself.

He studied his knuckles. "I do want you. I would rip that chemise off of you and take you again now. I don't think I'll ever get enough of you."

Thrills went through her. "Well, I… I feel the same."

He raised his gaze to hers. "I swore I wouldn't ask you again. It would be the very soul of idiocy for me to do so. I shan't do it. I shan't listen to you refuse me. But… I only want to say that you needn't choose, Lizzy, between me and your family. If you were my wife…"

She swallowed hard.

He searched her expression, and there was a such a vulnerability in his countenance that it seemed to physically cut her.

She tore her eyes away, feeling a lump rise in her throat.

"Anyway," he said, drawing himself up. "Consider it an open offer." He raised his chin. "I should like to see you tonight."

She smiled. "Yes. I should like that too."

CHAPTER TWENTY-ONE

Darcy couldn't concentrate on anything. He was supposed to be looking over the ledgers for some of the farms near Pemberley, but the numbers were swimming in front of his face, and all he could think about was Elizabeth.

He had not known it could be like that with a woman. He had never experienced anything like it. Before, he had always felt as if there was some barrier between him and whatever woman he was with. With women in his youth, it had been that they were more experienced than he and that they were only performing a service, lying beneath him and pretending to enjoy themselves. With Anne, it had been a wall of fear that he had tried to batter his way through rather than soothing her until she lowered it. He had lain with women before, had been inside them, but had never truly been inside, not until now.

Elizabeth had opened herself to him in a way that was so intimate it made him shudder. He felt a reverence toward it, toward her. He felt fortunate to have been gifted that secret part of her. He wanted her again. He was staggered by the ache he had for her. But he was stunned that he had even been allowed to have her in the first place.

Certainly, what they had shared, it couldn't be sordid and wicked. Perhaps she was his mistress in name, but the way they had been joined, it was something else, something almost magical and he—

"...sent him away, of course."

Darcy realized one of his footmen was talking to him.

"What?" he said, blinking at the boy.

"That Mr. Wickham you warned us about came to the door, but I sent him away."

"Oh," said Darcy. "Capital." Someone was finally listening to him.

"He said that I shouldn't have, that you would not want him spreading news around town about Mrs. Fieldstone and her family. Something about someone named Bennet, but I told him that you were taking risks now, and that you wouldn't have paid for his silence in any case."

Mr. Darcy felt a cold knife go through him. "You said what?"

The footman blinked, looking nervous. "Did I do the wrong thing, sir? Ought I have invited him in? Considering you did not return home until the morning—"

"Oh, dash it all," said Darcy, standing up. "What did he say? Did he say he would come back? Did he say that he would go and spread the story straightaway?"

"Well, he seemed drunk, sir."

"Oh, brilliant." Darcy massaged the bridge of his nose. "So, he would have had nothing to induce him to keep his mouth closed. Damn Wickham. *Damn* him."

* * *

The bad thing was that Darcy didn't know of any of Wickham's haunts anymore. Back when they had both been young, in the years during and after their shared schooling, he had known the taverns and places that Wickham liked to visit, but now, he was forced to go to various places that seemed as though they might please Wickham, which meant that his morning and much of his afternoon were taken up in fruitless inquiry.

But finally, he did find the man, though not in a tavern.

Instead, Wickham was wandering out of the back of one, buttoning his jacket, his hair askew and his cravat missing, looking for all the world as though he'd just woken up. When he saw Darcy, he gave him an insouciant grin. "Ah,

Darcy! What brings you to this part of the city?"

"Looking for you," Darcy said grimly. "I understand you came to my house last night."

"Indeed," said Wickham. "I was looking for you, but you weren't there."

"I had business to attend to," said Darcy.

"Oh, truly?" chortled Wickham. "Because I heard from everyone who I spoke of you to that you had been at a ball dancing with the mysterious Mrs. Fieldstone."

Darcy gritted his teeth. "Tell me that you did not say anything to anyone about Mrs. Fieldstone's true identity?"

"Why, of course I did." Wickham spread his hands. "How could I not? Your footman told me that you had no intention of paying me any more money, and that you didn't care what I blabbed about London."

Darcy felt an icy hand close over his spine.

Wickham laughed again and gave Darcy a little bow.

Darcy wanted to grab him by the throat and choke the life out of him. He didn't. "You utter..." Sputtering, he couldn't even find an insult worthy of him. "You have no idea what it is that you've done."

"I know *exactly* what I've done," said Wickham.

"You've ruined a woman who doesn't deserve it and cast aspersion on her innocent sisters. Not only that, you can't get any more money from me by blackmailing me to keep your mouth shut, so you've cut off your flow of currency there. All in all, I'd say that everyone loses, Wickham."

Wickham wrinkled up his nose, thinking about this. "Oh, well, perhaps... you know, I was so drunk, Darcy."

"How many people did you tell?"

"Anyone who would listen," said Wickham.

***

Elizabeth was sitting down for a light luncheon when she received another letter delivered by a servant, this one also from one of her sisters. But this one was not from Jane, but rather from Lydia. It was short. It simply stated that they must all meet at the home where Jane and the others resided and that calamity had struck.

Calamity? Elizabeth didn't like the sound of that. She wasn't even sure if she was welcome back under Jane's roof, but she hurried there as quickly as she could. When she got to the door, she was ushered inside by Kitty, whose face was white. She went into the parlor, where they were all assembled, even Lydia.

Lydia was pacing in front of the fireplace, in a brightly colored morning gown that was trimmed in miles of lace. Her face looked pinched.

Mary was sitting on the couch, her head bowed. She didn't look up when Elizabeth came in.

But Jane leapt out of her seat and ran to her, taking her hands. "Oh, Lizzy, you're here."

"What's happened?" said Elizabeth. "What calamity has struck?"

"It's all over town," said Lydia. "Everyone knows that I am, in fact, Lydia Bennet, and that you are not Mrs. Fieldstone but Elizabeth Bennet. They have all connected you to the business with Cumberbottom. It is so delicious a scandal that people will not cease talking about it for months and months, I fear. Possibly even all year. It is dreadful."

"Oh," said Elizabeth, turning to look at Mary. "Oh, I am so sorry."

"Yes, of course," Mary said drearily. "You offer your apologies, but you cannot stem the tide of woe that comes to us because of your transgressions."

"Oh, stop that, Mary," said Lydia, pacing more quickly. "No one wants to hear you quoting scripture."

"That was not scripture," said Mary. "That was my own words."

"Well, you read the bible too much, then," said Lydia. "Because you sound as though you are spouting scripture when you are not."

"You, my sister, are bound for hellfire," said Mary. "You must repent of your sins and beg for forgiveness—"

"Yes, yes," said Lydia. "Perhaps on my deathbed. But for now, we have other things to think of. It does not matter if my immortal soul is saved. It matters now that everyone in the family is ruined."

"We were already as good as ruined," Mary said.

"No, we weren't," burst out Kitty from the doorway, where she was hovering. "There was hope. After all, Mr. Bingley—"

"Oh, I had forgotten," said Lydia, turning on Jane. "Have you heard from him?"

"Well, he was here this morning," said Jane, but she looked ill. "However, it was only because he did not approve of Lizzy choosing to be Mr. Darcy's mistress instead of a life of propriety. He did not know that the news had spread all over town."

"You won't hear from him again," Lydia said.

"What?" said Elizabeth. "You think that Mr. Bingley will break his engagement? But to do so is monstrous."

"It is dishonorable to break an engagement, to be sure," said Lydia. "But how much more dishonorable is it to wed the sister of two notoriously loose women? His association with you, Jane, would be disastrous. He will break it off."

"Oh," said Jane, sitting down, her lower lip trembling.

"Lydia!" admonished Elizabeth.

"I am only telling the truth," said Lydia.

"You might have put it a bit more gently," Elizabeth said.

"There is no gentle way to put it," Lydia said. "This is the way of things. Now, I know that all of you had resisted coming to live with me before, but I think we must revisit that idea." She turned to Elizabeth. "You can take Mary and Jane, and I shall take Kitty."

"No," said Jane. "We won't do anything of the sort."

"I will not live in a house of ill repute," said Mary.

"There is no reason for you to stay in this dreadful

place," said Lydia. "There are no appearances to be kept up. Between Lizzy and I, we shall be able to keep everyone comfortable."

"And if one of us wants to strike out on her own and lie with men as well?" said Mary sharply. "I suppose you'll encourage our depravity to help put food on the table."

"Listen, Mary," said Lydia, "I know you have some idea in your head that what I do is sinful, but it is not. It is a double standard. Men are allowed to dally with whatever woman they choose, and they are not condemned for it."

"They are," countered Mary. "The Lord sees all, and he will judge on the last day."

"Well, anyway, it's not the same," said Lydia. "And I don't think it has anything to do with God or sin. It has to do with babies. Men don't like it when they can't be sure if a child is theirs or not. So, they keep women locked up in houses and teach them that it is sinful to give in to their natural desires, that they must fight what their own bodies want. But just because they say we must pass from our father's house to our husband's house with no time to understand who we are or to find our own way to love and to explore our emotions and our pleasures, that doesn't mean we have to listen. I am not a sinner. I am a woman doing my best. And if I happen to enjoy the freedoms that my station gives me, well, then, why shouldn't I?"

Mary flinched.

Jane blinked.

Elizabeth cocked her head at her sister. She didn't think she'd heard so much passion or intelligence come out of Lydia's mouth in... well, ever.

"I have not fallen," said Lydia. "I warrant my life is more full and more free than any wife's. I am my own. I belong to no one. That is my triumph."

Kitty licked her lips. "It sounds... lonely."

"Oh, does it?" said Lydia. "More lonely than what you have here? This sad little house, patching all your clothes, refusing to take too much money from me or Lizzy?"

"Well, we have each other," said Kitty.

It was quiet.

A long silence settled over all of the sisters.

Elizabeth looked out the window at the dirty street outside and she knew that she had been exposed, and that there were people out there talking about her, in much the same way as they had after the incident with Cumberbottom. Except, it would be worse this time, much worse. She felt a tremor at the thought of it, but… strangely… it didn't feel as bad as she thought it would. What did their words do to her, really? She was already cut off from their society. She had survived all this time without it. Perhaps, when she had refused Mr. Darcy —

"I don't think Bingley will break it off," Kitty suddenly burst out with. "I don't."

"He will," whispered Jane. "Lydia is right. He would have to wish himself ruin to marry me."

CHAPTER TWENTY-TWO

Dearest Fitzwilliam,

I know that we had plans to be together tonight, but I cannot do so. I am sorry, but matters have become rather grave, and I must spend the evening with my sisters. I suppose you must realize by now that I have been exposed. All of the city knows now that I am Mrs. Fieldstone, and they know what we have done together. It is a blow for you too, to have concealed your mistress, passed her off as someone respectable. But you will weather it easily. You are a man, and you are Mr. Darcy, master of Pemberley. It is different for you.

For us, we are devastated. And Jane especially is beside herself. We have not heard word from Mr. Bingley since all this happened. We fear the worst. He must break his engagement with Jane, because he cannot marry her now. We do understand it, but we are all deeply saddened. I feel it is especially hard on my sister, for she has suffered through so much with no respite. And now that something good has happened, it has been snatched away from her before she can enjoy it. It is not fair.

I cannot help but blame myself. I did not think of the others when I was with you last night. I was selfish, and I had no care for what might happen. I was brazen, and someone must have recognized me. I hear that Mrs. Heathspar, (the former Miss Bingley) is now back from her honeymoon. Perhaps it was her. Though I would not trade our night together for anything, I wish that I had not done this thing to hurt my sister so terribly.

I do not know when I will be able to see you again.
Please accept my apologies and my love.
Yours,

Lizzy

*　*　*

Dearest Lizzy,

You mustn't blame yourself for what occurred. In fact, it is unfortunately my fault that this has befallen your family. I know how your identity was discovered, and it was not because of Mrs. Heathspar. It was Mr. Wickham who did it. He came to my house last night while you and I were together, and he was turned away. He revealed your identity out of spite, because he is a blackguard and a villain. He has no care for anyone but himself.

It is my fault, though, because I had given my staff instructions to turn him away. Had I not done so, he might have been waiting for me this morning, and I might have paid him his money and your secret would still be safe. I am grieved when I think of my part in all of this. I have never wished ill to your sisters, and I am dreadfully sorry that this has all come about.

Please, take all the time you need to be with your sisters. If you are not so terribly angry with me that you will see me again, I shall be your willing servant whenever and wherever you wish.

With deepest apologies,
Fitzwilliam

*　*　*

Mr. Charles Bingley was not at all pleased to learn that not one but both of his sisters had come to visit him. He had not enjoyed even an entire month and a half of peace since Caroline had been married and moved away, and he would have been happy with many more weeks of silence before either one of them descended upon the house again. Surely, he would have done the courteous thing then, and invited them to dine with him. But until then, he would have liked not to have seen them at all.

It wasn't that he didn't love his sisters. He had an abundance of brotherly fondness for them. They were, of course, his only living family. He would do whatever it was that he could for them.

Luckily, he needed to do very little, since they were both married to respectable men now.

No, it wasn't a lack of love that made him despair of his sister's company, it was truly the fact that they talked too much. When it had only been Caroline at home, it had been a bit bearable, for Caroline had no one to converse with besides him, and he had chosen not to answer much of the time, which had meant that she would fall silent. But when they were both at home with him at the same time, they talked rather incessantly, and about all manner of things that were of no consequence, such as the color of bonnets or the thickness of the ribbon that trimmed a coat. They could converse on such a subject for hours. It was abominable.

Now, they were both here to see him. And it wasn't on a planned occasion, such as a dinner or a party. No, instead, they had just come to call upon him, both at once. A servant had come to tell him so, and now he stood frozen, reeling from the news. His sisters were both in his sitting room at that very moment.

What was it that they could possibly want?

It must be about Miss Bennet.

He had sent word to them both, by letter, that he was going to marry. He expected neither of them would be pleased about it. After all, they had not liked Miss Bennet when he had first met her, deeming her connections too inferior for him. But he thought that his sisters were both largely motivated by attempting to raise themselves in society and thought that their brother's diminishment might harm their station. But now, they were more well known by their connections to their husbands than their connections to him. He did not see it as an issue. Even if it was, it was his business, not theirs, and he would do as he pleased.

Of course, he had sent them word before the news had broken all over London of Miss Elizabeth and Miss Lydia. Now, everyone knew of all the sordidness of the Bennet clan. Now, all was changed.

That did not mean he wished to listen to his sisters babble about such things. But he could not very well cast them out into the streets. They were his relations, and he had no choice but to go and greet them.

So, he did just that. On his way, he stopped in to ask the housekeeper to make sure that an abundance of cakes and biscuits might be brought up to the sitting room. If his sisters were chewing, they could not be talking, at least that was what he reckoned.

When he entered the room, Louisa and Caroline both stood. They were both wearing white dresses trimmed with pale colored ribbons. They both had furrows in their brow as if something terrible had happened, like a death in the family. Caroline was actually wringing her hands.

"Oh, dear, Charles," said Louisa. "What a pickle you have gotten yourself into."

"You have to break the engagement," said Caroline.

He strode through the room and went to a chair and sat down.

They both sat down on couches that flanked him, crossing their legs and leaning close to him.

"You mustn't worry that there will be any legal repercussions," said Caroline. "You weren't so foolish as to put it in writing, were you?"

"Even if you were, it is not likely that the Bennet family would be able to bring suit," said Louisa.

"Well, they do seem to have all the money flowing in through Miss Swan," said Caroline. "Have you *seen* the dresses she wears to the opera?"

"Yes, I've heard that a man must buy her jewelry just to have an audience with her," said Louisa.

"Why do men want women like her?" said Caroline. "I can't understand it. She is used and damaged goods. It makes no sense to me why any man would pay to be with a courtesan when he has a good and proper wife at home who has kept herself virtuous for him."

"Yes, it is abominable," said Louisa. "Men are so horrid." She looked at her brother. "Except you, Charles. We all know that you would never be associated with such a practice."

"Which is why you will break the engagement," said Caroline. "In all truth, you should never have asked for her hand in the first place. Lord, I cannot understand what it is that you see in that woman. She is the lowest of the low."

" Sweet, of course, " said Louisa. " A very sweet personality."

"Oh, to be sure," said Caroline. "It is almost a pity she was saddled with such sisters."

" But it must be the fault of the parents, do you not think?" said Louisa. "Why that mother of hers, I heard that she racked up debt before keeling over, and she conducted herself in a most improper manner on every occasion that we met with her. Why, I think it positively miraculous that the eldest Miss Bennet ever could comport herself with any civility at all with such a guiding hand in her formative years."

"Oh, I wholeheartedly agree, sister."

"Of course you do. Anyone would."

"Indeed."

"Indeed."

They both turned to look at Bingley.

He looked back and forth between them. "Are you quite done?"

" Well, we haven't had much to say," said Caroline. "Only that you—"

"Must break off the engagement with Miss Bennet," said Bingley. "Yes, I have heard you. Is there anything else you wish to say?"

" Are you going to break it off?" said Louisa. "I really think you must."

Bingley rubbed his chin. " Well, I hear what you are saying."

"And you offer no argument?" said Caroline.

"I do not," said Bingley.

"Oh, dear, thank goodness," said Louisa. "I thought we'd have to wrestle you kicking and screaming to our way of thinking."

A maid entered the room with a platter of cakes.

Bingley gestured. " Perhaps you'd care for some refreshment?"

***

Elizabeth sent a letter back to Mr. Darcy telling him that she did not blame him for what Wickham had done. It was no one's fault, truly, but she could not help but feel as though the punishments for her transgressions were being visited on her sisters, and she was sorry for it.

She did inform her sisters about what had happened, and Lydia seemed aghast when she heard that Wickham had done it.

"I shall skin him alive," said Lydia. "No, I shall bar him from entering my house. That would show him. He cannot live without me."

Elizabeth knew that Lydia cared about the plight of her sisters, but in all truth, Lydia was the least affected by the news. She had already been Miss Lydia Swan, the famous courtesan. Nothing had been done to change her reputation. Elizabeth would have liked to think that Lydia would punish Wickham, but she didn't really expect her to. Lydia and Wickham had that strange bond that Elizabeth couldn't understand.

She could not term it love, though they had been connected for many years now, because they both seemed so willing to share the other with a multitude of others. That couldn't be love, or if it was, it was a love that Elizabeth didn't understand. And for all that, Wickham was a horrible person. But when Jane said something similar, calling Wickham names, Lydia agreed. And then took it back.

"He is awful," Lydia sighed. "But he simply doesn't think things through. He has no conception of consequences. He lives entirely in the present moment, and he... well, he can be a great deal of fun sometimes." Lydia sighed wistfully.

"Fun?" said Jane, aghast.

"Jane," admonished Elizabeth. "Let it be." There was nothing that could be said that would sever things between Wickham and Lydia. Elizabeth knew this to be true.

Jane was trying desperately to concentrate on some embroidery, but she should not as she kept having to rip up her stitches and start over because she was making horrendous mistakes. "I don't know what to do. Should I attempt to contact Mr. Bingley? Should I force his hand? If he has truly jilted me, I should like to know. I *deserve* to know."

"Well, he *has* jilted you," said Lydia.

"Shut up, Lydia," said Kitty.

"Perhaps if I send him a letter, however," said Jane, "it will only unsettle him worse and make him more inclined to wish to be rid of me."

"No one could wish to be rid of you," said Elizabeth.

"Except Mr. Bingley," muttered Jane. "No, if it is like last time, I do not think I can bear it. To see him nearly every day, and then for him to simply be gone and never to hear from him again... I will break if it happens again. I will fall apart."

"You will not break," said Elizabeth. "You are strong. And if that is what Mr. Bingley does, you are well shut of him. If he breaks off your engagement, he is a weak-willed, lily-livered sort of man who doesn't deserve you. He did not fight for you before. He allowed Mr. Darcy to talk him out of marrying you and was too schooled by the words of his sisters. Now, if he does the same thing, you will have lost nothing, because there is no use for a man like that in your life, Jane. You will be better off without him."

Elizabeth meant her words to bolster Jane and lift her spirits, but Jane burst into tears and fled from the room.

"Oh, nicely done, Lizzy," said Mary dryly.

Elizabeth buried her face in her hands.

CHAPTER TWENTY-THREE

Mr. Darcy rapped on the door of Mr. Bingley's home. He had not called here in quite some time. He and Bingley used to be much closer, but they had drifted apart in the ensuing years. He still considered him a good friend, but he had not been to see him in what seemed like a very, very long time.

The butler opened the door and informed him that Mr. Bingley was not at home.

Except that Mr. Darcy could hear Mr. Bingley speaking from within the house. He was giving instructions to someone about what to do with a large amount of leftover biscuits.

Well, so it was that way, then. Darcy knew that Bingley had not approved of his arrangement with Elizabeth, but he did not expect his friend to cut him out so insistently. But it was obvious that Bingley did not want to see him. Darcy gave the butler a sharp nod and then turned to go down the steps.

That was when he noticed that Bingley's carriage was waiting on the street.

Just at that moment, the door opened, and Bingley came out, holding his hat. "Oh," he said. "Darcy!"

"Bingley," said Darcy, nodding back. "I know that you do not wish to speak to me. I shall honor that. I was just on my way—"

"I did not know it was you at the door," said Bingley. "I am on my way out, as you can see. If you have something you wish to say to me briefly, then out with it."

"Oh," said Darcy, who was now understanding the way it must have gone. Since Bingley was preparing to leave, he had instructed the servants to turn away any callers. It had not been personal after all. "Well…" He smiled. "Well, good, then. I am glad to hear it."

"To hear what?" Bingley was confused. "I say, Darcy, I am in a bit of a hurry, so if you don't mind—"

"I'll be brief, then," said Darcy. "I am here to plead on the behalf of Miss Bennet."

"Miss Elizabeth?" said Bingley.

" No, the eldest Miss Bennet. Your intended, as I understand."

"And you are here on her behalf? You, who discouraged me from forming an alliance with her in the first place?"

" Well, yes, that was … I am sorry for that. I feel as though I have already apologized when we spoke of this before."

"Perhaps you did. I have to admit I am confused. You obviously do not feel the family is of the proper standards to make an alliance with one of the women in it. You have reduced all of them by the way you have treated Miss Elizabeth."

Darcy looked away, feeling ashamed. " Yes, I will not deny it." True, he had asked Elizabeth to marry him, but it had been too late. He had done it after he had wrecked her reputation and compromised her in all the ways that mattered. And now he had taken her completely and thoroughly. It was done, and he was whatever Bingley thought of him. He would take responsibility for himself. He would not make petty excuses.

"It is shameful," said Bingley.

"Indeed," Darcy allowed, glancing up at Bingley. "Even so, if there is any way that I could prevail upon you to honor your engagement to Miss Bennet, I would entreat you to do so. If you would but marry her, the effect on both of the younger Bennet sisters would be such that—"

"Oh, this is why you have come?" said Bingley.

"I said I'd come on her behalf."

"Yes, now I see what you mean," said Bingley. "Well, you might have saved yourself a trip, truly. There is nothing I need to hear on that subject. I have quite made up my mind."

* * *

Elizabeth flung the door open to see that both Mr. Bingley and Mr. Darcy were outside of their house.

"Miss Elizabeth," said Mr. Bingley.

Darcy looked her over and there was heat in his expression. "Miss Elizabeth," he said, but the tone of his voice sent shivers through her.

She pressed her lips together, trying to keep her composure, and let them both into the house.

Bingley did not wait for an invitation, but went directly into the sitting room.

"You look well," said Mr. Darcy. He had not taken his eyes off of her.

She looked up at him, her pulse thrumming beneath her skin. "As do you," she murmured. She wanted to touch him. Lord, she wanted to touch him. Could it have only been last night that they had been entangled in her bed, nothing between them except the thin French letter?

Bingley stalked back out. "Where is Jane?"

Elizabeth did not think she had ever heard her sister's first name come out of his lips. He looked out of sorts, however. Perhaps he was breaking down, unable to keep himself at his normal level of decorum.

But before Elizabeth could answer, Jane came running out from her bedroom, her face still wet with tears. "Mr. Bingley?" she breathed. "You are... are here?"

"Why, of course," he said. "I would have come earlier, but I was pestered with a steady stream of visitors. First my sisters and then Mr. Darcy. I have been quite occupied and not the least bit pleased about it."

"Oh," said Jane. "I see. Then you are not...? That is, you have not come in person to... to..."

"How are you, my dearest?" Bingley went to her, gathering her into his arms. "I am so sorry you have been left here to deal with this disastrous news alone. I should have been by your side all along."

"You should have?" Jane smiled at him. "Truly? Then you are not going to jilt me?"

"Jilt you?" said Bingley. "Never."

"But this changes things now. You will be ignored. Even your own sisters may refuse to associate with you," said Jane.

"We shall form our own society," said Bingley, brushing her hair behind her ear. "You are the only one I care to be near, anyway."

Elizabeth was smiling too. She could see the look in her sister's eyes, and the way that Bingley was staring back, and she took Mr. Darcy's hand and pulled him out of the hallway and into the parlor so that Bingley and Jane might have a moment together alone. She was rather sure that Mr. Bingley was about to kiss her sister.

"What is going on?" said Lydia when they entered the room.

"It's Mr. Bingley," said Elizabeth. "He is not going to break the engagement."

"I knew he wouldn't," said Kitty, sighing happily.

Lydia looked stunned. "Well, I... am surprised. Who would have thought it of Bingley?" Then she noticed Mr. Darcy. "Oh, hello."

Darcy inclined his head. "Miss Lydia. I hope you are well."

"Yes, indeed," said Lydia. "And you as well."

Mary got up to stare daggers at Mr. Darcy. "Well, it is a good thing that there is one man with honor in our house."

"Mary!" said Elizabeth. "How dare you?"

"No, it is all understandable," said Mr. Darcy. He cleared

his throat. "I shall take my leave, since all is well, or at least better than it has been."

"Yes," said Elizabeth. "I suppose that would be best. But perhaps we can now renew our plans for the night."

"Oh, certainly. That would be most agreeable," said Mr. Darcy. He winked at her.

She blushed. She seemed to feel it all over.

CHAPTER TWENTY-FOUR

Elizabeth let out a satisfied sigh. She felt like a preening cat, groomed and happy. She stretched her neck and flung her arms out on the bed.

Mr. Darcy was still inside her. His forehead was buried next to hers in the pillow, and he was panting.

"That felt... different," Elizabeth murmured. "I don't know. It was as though I could feel you better there at the end. I don't know what I mean by that. It's a strange to say."

"No, I agree." He lifted his head to gaze down at her. "It was... somehow different. Better. More..." He kissed her.

She opened her mouth to him and the kiss was deep and thorough and lovely.

He sighed too, and then rolled away from her, lying on his back next to her. "I don't know why I put up such a fight about this. It has all been—" He made a funny, half-strangled sound.

"What?" she said, sitting up. "What's wrong?"

Mr. Darcy pointed at himself, at his male organ, which was soft now, but still intriguing. She was unsure about touching it still, but she thought that she would have the courage to do it soon. She mused on that for a moment, but then forced herself back to the present. "I still don't understand," she said.

"The French letter," said Darcy, turning to look at her. "It's not there."

"Oh," said Elizabeth, now very worried. "Well, where is it?" She thrust a hand between her own thighs and found it.

Except it was torn, useless. It had not done its job.

Darcy snatched it from her, emitting a low moan. "Bloody hell."

"Mr. Darcy, the swearing," said Elizabeth, sitting up. "Well... what does that mean?"

"It means," said Darcy, his voice harsh, "that I've quite likely gotten you with child, and that now you will have to bring it into the world and probably die in the attempt, and when I lose you, I shall kill myself, because I don't want to live without you."

"Fitzwilliam, heavens." She let out a laugh. "You are being very dire. We don't even know if I'm with child."

"There was nothing stopping it," said Darcy. "My seed has been sown."

"Oh, don't say that," said Elizabeth. "It's so ... agricultural."

He got up out of bed and began pulling on his clothes.

"What are you doing?" she said.

"I don't know. I need to walk," he said. "I need some air. I need something." He thrust his hands in his hair and turned in a circle. "Dear God, Lizzy, this is the worst thing that could have happened."

She bit down on her lip. "Look, even if I am with child, I think the odds are good that I'm not going to *die*, Fitzwilliam."

He swallowed, pulling his shirt over his head. "No, you're right. I won't let you. I will have every accoucheur in the country attending you. You will stay in bed for the entire nine months. And there will be no strenuous activity of any kind. Nothing to risk your health."

"In bed for how long? You're being silly. I will deliver the babe just fine. I am a strong, sturdy, healthy woman. Fitzwilliam, I am not Anne."

"I know that," he said. "I survived losing her. I will not survive losing you."

"You won't lose me," she said. But after the babe was

born, then what? Who would their child be, but Mr. Darcy's natural child? Her child would not inherit anything, would not make a good marriage, would not have any future at all. She felt her throat tighten.

"I'm going for a walk," Darcy said, shrugging into his jacket.

"Yes," she said quietly. "Perhaps that would be a good idea."

* * *

Elizabeth slept alone that night. Mr. Darcy did not come back. She would have been more upset about that if it hadn't been for the fact that she was consumed with thoughts of her unborn child's lack of a proper future.

Lord, had she been an idiot?

Or just selfish?

It must be that. She had worried about the fact that she'd be ridiculed by women, and she had run from being Darcy's wife, and look what had happened. She had been exposed anyway. Her name would be dragged through the mud regardless. Her sisters had been tarnished as well. All of it was for naught. She was ashamed of herself. Now, her sweet innocent babe would suffer, all in the name of what?

She could not allow this to happen.

The next morning, she ate breakfast quickly and then dressed to go and call on Mr. Darcy. It was scandalous for her to call on him on her own, of course, but she had done it before, and she was now no stranger to scandal.

Before she could leave, however, a letter arrived from Darcy. It contained a recipe for a tea that his housekeeper had apparently given him. The tea was meant to induce a miscarriage.

Appalled, Elizabeth ripped the letter into shreds and called for a coach.

When she got to Mr. Darcy's house, she did not wait for him in the sitting room, but instead went tearing through the house to the chagrin of the servants. She went to his study, where she threw open the door and cried, "What do you take me for?"

Darcy was in his banyan, sitting by the window, looking as though he had not slept. He stood up, gaping at her.

"How could you possibly send me that awful tea recipe?" she demanded. "You can't think that I would do such a thing, can you? To do away with our own child? What kind of woman do you think I am?"

He just stared at her, his lips parted.

She advanced on him, across the room, closing the distance between them. "I could never do that."

He closed his mouth and he averted his eyes. "All I can think about is losing you. I *can't* lose you."

"You have to face that fear, Fitzwilliam," she said. "And I have to face mine. I have been such a hypocrite, urging you to do things that terrify you and then refusing to do the same myself. And when I thought of what might happen to a child that I would deliver out of the bonds of marriage, I began to wonder what sort of idiotic selfish creature I had become."

He furrowed his brow. "What are you saying?"

"You said that it was an open offer, did you not?"

He looked confused for a moment, but then it dawned upon him. He raised his eyebrows. "Wait, are you saying…?"

She took a deep breath and gave him a wobbly smile. "Can you possibly bear an idiotic selfish creature such as me for a wife?"

He chuckled softly. "Can you possibly bear a coward like me for a husband?"

"Oh, Fitzwilliam, you are not a coward."

"And you are neither an idiot nor selfish, but the best woman that I know. And if we were to be married, you would make me the happiest man alive."

Her smile strengthened. "Oh, I want to marry you."

"Are you certain?"

" Yes, I am. I am indeed. One wonders how much suffering might have been avoided if I had simply accepted you in the first place all those years ago."

"Well, as you pointed out at the time, I rather made a mess of that proposal."

"You did," she said. "But I was too ensconced in my own pride to see my own faults. It seems to be a bit of a habit with me. Here I have been doing the same thing. Scolding you for something I myself have not conquered."

"Oh, Miss Bennet... cease your wagging tongue and kiss me."

She laughed more, and then they were in each other's arms.

CHAPTER TWENTY-FIVE

For Elizabeth, the prospect of the babe was no worry now that she and Mr. Darcy were engaged. Of course, they needed to be wedded with all haste, but that was no trouble, for they could marry in the same ceremony as Jane and Mr. Bingley, who were happy to share the joy of their day with the other couple. Bingley was most relieved, and he said that it would all be more bearable if they could call on each other. Even if the rest of society deserted them, they would have their own circle.

Jane said later that she thought he was simply happy to have Mr. Darcy to talk to as opposed to all the women.

Elizabeth said that he could have spoken to Mr. Darcy regardless, and Jane agreed, but she said that he wasn't speaking to him on principle, because he thought that Darcy had treated Elizabeth so poorly.

At which point Elizabeth felt compelled to explain to her sister that it was she who had refused Mr. Darcy's marriage proposal. She explained her fear of being talked about and noticed.

Jane did not condemn her. That was not her way. She only said that she was happy that Elizabeth had changed her mind. And that Mr. Darcy had taken his time in coming to ask for her hand in the first place, so he still deserved some censure.

That all aside, Elizabeth was happy for her future. Truthfully, even though she was being talked about all over London, she did not know, because no one would dare associate with her to say it to her face. As for the papers, she did not read them.

But Mr. Darcy was still in quite a bad way about the prospect of Elizabeth being with child. He tried to have her to go and see an accoucheur, but she told him that they must wait and see if her courses appeared before they had any fear of that.

One week before the wedding, she began to bleed.

She was relieved. She knew that Mr. Darcy would be relieved too.

But strangely, it was bittersweet, as if she had lost something too. She had not realized that she had grown attached to the idea of her own child, of a family with Mr. Darcy. But she was, and she wanted that. That was how she knew she had made the right choice to marry him. It wasn't only because she had fallen for him or because she liked the way his hands felt on her skin. They had the foundations here for something deep and everlasting.

She told Mr. Darcy when he came to call on her the following day. Now that they were engaged, they had decided not to keep her house and not to spend any more nights together. Mr. Darcy was driven in that by the fear of getting her with child if he had not, but also because they wanted to wait until their wedding night to be together again.

So, Mr. Darcy called on her at the small house she still shared with her sisters and they were able to steal a few moments alone by sending the others out into the dining room.

"I am not with child," she told him.

His eyes widened. "No?" He breathed a sigh of relief, a smile spreading over his face. "But this is good news. This is very, very good news." He kissed her.

She kissed him for a minute and then pushed him away. She wasn't comfortable with too many kisses too close to where her sisters might peek in and see. It wasn't proper.

"You shouldn't be so happy about it. I could have been carrying the heir to Pemberley and—"

"I don't want heirs, I want you," he said, shaking his head.

"Well, perhaps you can have both," she said, putting her hand on his cheek.

"Ah, I don't know," he said. "That's taking a risk."

"Well, Fitzwilliam," she said, "that is what we do."

CHAPTER TWENTY-SIX

Elizabeth and Jane had almost decided to forgo a wedding breakfast, because they did not think anyone would come, but Kitty had been so put out by the thought of not having it that they had decided to have the breakfast after all, and they held it at Mr. Darcy's home, because he could accommodate more people if anyone actually did arrive.

Since no one was coming anyway, Elizabeth invited Lydia, because she wanted her sister to be there on their day of celebration. She wanted her whole family to be together. And Lydia came, with Wickham in tow, of all people, and Elizabeth didn't know what to do about that. She was half-inclined to have him thrown out. She thought maybe Mr. Darcy might. After all, Georgiana was there, and why should he be allowed to be near her? That might upset her greatly.

But Georgiana seemed to pay Wickham no mind, because she was absorbed with playing a most complicated piece on the piano. She only paused briefly for a few bites of wedding cake, and then said that she would like to play for them all, that the music would be her gift to her brother, because she wished him such happiness.

In the end, they let Wickham stay. He seemed subdued in the company of Lydia anyway, as if she was able to rein him in.

Elizabeth still found the two of them puzzling, she had to admit. But Lydia was not going to change her lifestyle.

She was ensconced. And what was more, Elizabeth rather thought her sister was happy. Who was she to say that Lydia should live any differently?

The strangest of arrivals was that of Charlotte Lucas — Mrs. Collins now. Elizabeth was not even sure how Mrs. Collins had gotten wind of the breakfast, but she arrived, with her husband in tow, who began talking of ridiculous things to anyone who would listen. He had never approved of the fact that his wife had kept in touch with Elizabeth after her reputation had been smeared. After all, Lady Catherine had used her influence to get him to boot them out of Longbourn as soon as was legally possible.

But Charlotte had always been strong and determined. She had never shunned her old friend. And she was somehow able to influence Mr. Collins to go along with it all. Why, they even brought their two children, both girls.

Charlotte embraced Elizabeth and wished her all the happiness in the world. "I always thought you liked Mr. Darcy, no matter what you said."

Elizabeth laughed. "Oh, I did not. I hated him."

"You were far too out of sorts about the fact that he called you tolerable," said Charlotte.

"What?" said Mr. Darcy, coming over with a drink to hand to Elizabeth. "What are you talking about?"

"Oh, nothing," said Elizabeth.

Mr. Darcy gave her the drink. "Tolerable," he repeated softly. Then his eyes widened. "You *heard* me?"

Elizabeth giggled.

Charlotte giggled.

Elizabeth put her nose in her drink.

"Oh, Lord," said Darcy. "Well, no wonder you said no the first time I proposed."

"I suppose I grew on you," said Elizabeth, smiling.

"Oh, don't be silly," he said. "You know how I hate to dance with strangers. I would have said anything to get out of that." He put his arm around her. And then he smiled at

Charlotte. "Mrs. Collins. So good of you to come."

"Oh, of course," said Charlotte.

"How did you even—" But Elizabeth broke off because someone else had been escorted in by a servant, a person she had never expected to see again in her entire life.

Lady Catherine.

The elderly woman made her way into the room, holding herself upright and looking about with a severe expression on her face.

"Oh, dear," said Mr. Darcy.

"It was from Lady Catherine we heard," said Charlotte. "When I said that we would come, she said she thought that was a capital idea."

"You still speak to Lady Catherine?" said Elizabeth.

"Oh, she dotes on Mr. Collins," said Charlotte. "Invites us to visit several times a year. I think she is lonely, truly. She has no one now, after what happened to her daughter. And, uh, well, she does have not the personality that tends to, er, ingratiate her to many."

Elizabeth laughed.

Darcy patted Elizabeth on the arm. "I will deal with her. You stay here." He moved away to intercept Lady Catherine, who was making a beeline for Elizabeth.

But Lady Catherine could not be intercepted. She waved her nephew off and was soon standing right in front of Elizabeth.

"Mrs. Darcy," she said. "You look well."

"Thank you, Lady Catherine," said Elizabeth. "You look well also."

"I do not," said Lady Catherine. "What I look, primarily, is old. I have outlived all my siblings and my own child. So, since I am so old, I may have very little time left. I shall get straight to the point."

Elizabeth steeled herself for it. This was the woman who had arranged for her to be kissed by Cumberbottom, who had manipulated her and set her life on its ruinous course.

She did not want to hear what awful things she was going to say on her wedding day. Forget Wickham, Lady Catherine should be forced to leave, on today of all days.

"I am sorry," said Lady Catherine.

Elizabeth sputtered. "What? You are what?"

"I can't say that I didn't have good reasons for what I did. And I have my excuses as well. But in the end, I have reaped the wages of my sins, because in one day I lost both my daughter and the only grandchild I would ever have."

Elizabeth felt a sudden stab of sympathy for the woman. She *was* alone, wasn't she? "My sincere condolences, Lady Catherine. That must have been an awful day for you."

Lady Catherine drew in a breath. "Sometimes, I have pondered what would have happened if I had not left things well enough alone. If, then, my daughter might not still be alive. After all, it seems that you and my nephew have come together after all, despite quite a large amount of obstacles in your path, many of them put there by my own actions. And you are happy. If I had not meddled, what might have been?"

"We do not know that, madam."

"No, we do not," said Lady Catherine. "But I want you to know that I do not fault you for the choices you have made. When I think of the options you had before you, I know you must have done as best as you could. And now, you are married, so it hardly matters."

"Truly?" Elizabeth was quite surprised by this. She had not expected that Lady Catherine would bend in terms of propriety. She seemed the soul of rigidity.

"Truly," said Lady Catherine. "It would be hypocrisy to blame you when I am at fault."

"Well…"

"No, do not protest. It *is* my fault. I am the one who set it all in motion. And I regret it. I find that when I think of your future, I do not wish to have any more of my family gone from me, not if there is something I can do to keep them close. So, I have come to ask for forgiveness."

"It is the past, Lady Catherine," Elizabeth found herself saying immediately. "You must not let yourself think on it any longer." It was odd. She could not have dreamed of forgiving this woman even an hour earlier, but now she could not see why she should cause anyone pain. Even Lady Catherine.

"You are kind," said Lady Catherine, looking at her with what Elizabeth might term respect. "I know it may come as a shock, but I always rather liked you."

Elizabeth's eyebrows shot up.

"It's true," said Lady Catherine. "You are a woman with backbone, and you are not afraid to speak your mind. I admire such attributes. I do not deserve to trespass on your goodwill further, but I must ask. I should like it if... you and my nephew, when you have children, will you bring them to Rosings sometimes? Will you allow me to dote on them, treat them as the grandchildren that I might have had otherwise? I know it is a lot to ask, and you may say no, or you may say that you will think on it, and I shall not press further."

"I shall say yes," said Elizabeth. "For without you, our children shall have no grandparents at all."

Lady Catherine's hand shot out and she grasped Elizabeth's. Her eyes shone. "Thank you. You have made me happier today than I have been in quite some time."

Elizabeth smiled at the woman. It was strange how she had gone from fearing and despising the woman to feeling pity for her. Perhaps people were often cruel because they needed pity. Elizabeth did not know, but she had to admit that letting go of the anger that she had felt toward Lady Catherine had healed something in her that she didn't even know was broken.

Lady Catherine let go of Elizabeth's hand and moved on.

Darcy rushed to her side. He kept his voice low. "Are you quite mad? You have promised to visit her? You do remember what she's like, don't you?"

She laughed. "Oh, Fitzwilliam, we have so little family left. We must keep close to as many as we can. Society may shun us, but I will shun no one." She sighed. "We have even allowed Wickham to come to our wedding breakfast."

"Yes, but that is only because we are stupendously happy," said Mr. Darcy. "And the moment that he asks for money, I shall hit him, I really shall."

"I don't think you would hit him."

"He could do with a good blow to the nose," said Darcy, peering through the people in the room at Wickham. "I think it would be good for him."

"No one is hitting anyone on my wedding day," said Elizabeth, lifting her chin. "Promise me, Fitzwilliam."

"Oh, very well," he said, smiling at her. "I would do nothing to displease you, not on my life."

And soon, they were all seated at the long table in the dining room, and Georgiana's music served as a lovely undercurrent to their conversation and laughter. The food was delicious, the future was bright, and they were all together.

At long last, Elizabeth thought, there was nothing to fear.

CHAPTER TWENTY-SEVEN

one-and-a-half years later...
"I do not care what you say. That man has to leave," said Mr. Billingsworth, the accoucheur that was attending Elizabeth in her labor. Well, the only one who had lasted throughout the pregnancy, that is, for Mr. Darcy had proven to be irrationally concerned about his wife while she was increasing, to the point that one after another, every accoucheur and midwife excused themselves, saying they could not bear to listen to the man anymore.

If Darcy ' d had his way, the room would have been packed full with ten or more attendants, all there simply to make sure that everything was going well. But all had left except Mr. Billingsworth, even the aging midwife from Pemberley who had attended the births of Darcy children for three generations. She had thrown up her hands in disgust at the thought of Mr. Darcy being in the birthing chamber.

Elizabeth was lying back on the bed, exhausted. She had been in labor for a very long time now. She thought it had been days, but she was not sure how many. She knew that she had not slept, and that it had been dark and then light and then dark again. She was in pain now, rather a lot, although the pain had not been nearly as bad as she had worried it was going to be earlier in the process. Rather, the experience had been difficult largely because it seemed interminable, and because the contractions would not allow her to sleep for longer than a few moments at a time.

"I'm not leaving!" Darcy cried. He had been banished to the corner some time ago, over his own protests, but Elizabeth had thought it better. She didn't mind that Darcy was there. In fact, she was rather glad of his presence. The fact that he was here, going through it all with her, was very comforting. But at this point, Elizabeth was very close to the edge of some precipice of madness. It was the lack of rest, she thought. Or the incessant pain. She did not know.

"You!" Billingsworth turned, wagging his finger at Darcy. "You are not to speak. We agreed you would shut your mouth."

"You must let me hold her hand," Darcy protested. "She needs me."

Elizabeth gritted her teeth as pain ripped through her. She wanted to get up and walk, but she was too tired to move. She wanted to push this babe out of her body now, but everyone kept telling her it wasn't time yet, and she was so exhausted. She would not have the strength to do it when the time came.

"Mrs. Darcy," said Billingsworth, turning back to her. "I am taking your husband out of the room."

"No," said Elizabeth, gasping. "No, he wants to stay. You won't be able to force him to leave." At this point, Elizabeth did not care. She was feeling an incredible pressure in her pelvis, and it was unbearable. She needed to get up somehow.

"I have told him you are not going to die," said Billingsworth. "I have explained to him—"

"You do not know!" Darcy cried. "You cannot predict the future."

Billingsworth turned on his heel and stalked over to the corner. "Listen, Mr. Darcy, you hired me for my expertise in delivering children, did you not?"

Elizabeth grabbed onto the bed post and, groaning, pulled herself up into a position that was sort of a squat. It was agony, but it was somehow better than the other position she'd been in. Blinding pain ripped through her, but she didn't cry out. Sometimes crying out made it worse. Sometimes, it was better to breathe.

"Yes," said Darcy. "But that does not mean that you are God Almighty, Billingsworth."

Elizabeth clutched the bed post and bore down, pushing instinctively. She didn't know what she was doing, but she knew that she needed to do this. Her body was demanding that she do this.

"You know my credentials, sir," said Billingsworth. "Will you force me to list them again?"

Elizabeth rested for a moment, gasping for air. No, she couldn't rest. She had to *push* again.

"Nothing you say will induce me to leave the room."

"Husbands are not to be in the birthing chamber," said Billingsworth. "It is not done."

Elizabeth pushed again, and now there was the worst pain she had ever experienced, a sort of burning ring inside her. And yet, she had to push through the pain, she knew she must, and she could do nothing but push. She grunted.

"Mrs. Darcy?" Billingsworth was rushing back across the room to her.

Elizabeth kept pushing, crying out, screaming in effort.

Billingsworth was gathering her skirts out of the way. "Oh, yes, Mrs. Darcy, very good. There you are, that's perfect."

Elizabeth was sobbing. She rested for a moment before she knew she had to push again, but this time, Billingsworth was there, pulling her babe free. Its cry pierced the room, and Elizabeth didn't think that she'd ever heard anything so lovely in her entire life.

Darcy was coming across the room. "You did it." He stopped next to Billingsworth. "She did it," he said in an amazed voice.

Elizabeth's entire body was jelly.

"It's a boy," murmured Billingsworth.

"Oh, good," said Elizabeth, gazing up at her husband.

"He's beautiful," said Mr. Darcy. "Just perfect. You..." Then he turned to her, alarmed. "You are all right?"

"Yes," whispered Elizabeth. "I am all right." And she reached up her arms for her baby.

* * *

For a long time afterward, Elizabeth didn't want to let go of her new little son. She did anyway, because she had to let her husband hold the baby. And when Jane and Kitty and Mary came in, she had to let them hold the baby too. Jane's little girl Laura was only a year old and not old enough to hold the baby, but still very curious about him all the same.

Elizabeth was happy.

She and Mr. Darcy had retired to Pemberley for the most part, leaving the bustle of London behind since they were never invited anywhere anymore. Kitty had come to live with them and Mary had gone to stay with Jane and Bingley, who lived not too far away at Bingley's country estate. Mary could not bear to be around Elizabeth, who was still too mired in iniquity for her taste.

Though there were plenty in the country who would not have a thing to do with them, there was a local parson who called frequently, Mr. Whittaker, although he seemed primarily interested in speaking with Kitty, who was equally enamored with him.

Jane and Bingley were less shunned, and they even received a few invitations to balls in the country at other's homes. Jane said that Mary had been dancing rather regularly with a very respectable man named Mr. Bartlett, who didn't even seem to mind Mary's sermonizing.

Georgiana came to visit regularly, and when she did, she always seemed happy to have her freedom. She never seemed wistful for dances or the prospect of marriage. Even now, holding her new, tiny nephew, she said that she thought he was quite perfect, but she was glad that she would never have a child, because she would not know what to do with one. "It's such a relief to give him back," she said, laughing.

Elizabeth was happy to take him back. She did not want to let go of him. He was so tiny and perfect and wonderful, and she was amazed by all the things about him that were so detailed and flawless. His little fingernails. His tiny lips. His blinking, confused eyes. He seemed happiest close to her, as if he was not too pleased about having been removed from inside her body. Truly, he had taken his time coming out, after all.

Finally, everyone had seen the baby and it was just Elizabeth and Fitzwilliam and their son.

He sat behind her on the bed and she leaned into his chest, and he wrapped his arms around them both.

"That was wretched," he said.

"Was it?" She couldn't help but laugh.

"You enjoyed it?"

"No, of course not, but, well, now we have this little one."

"Yes, that's true." Fitzwilliam's hand smoothed over their son's head, and it was touching to see his thick fingers give such a gentle caress. "Still, I am in no hurry to do that again any time soon."

She looked at him, smiling. "But you *do* want to do it again, don't you?"

"I…" He looked down at her and then planted a kiss on her forehead. "It is as you say, Lizzy. Some things are worth the risk."

Thanks so much for reading!

I love to get reviews. I read each and every one.

Look for my other P&P variations:
Escape with Mr. Darcy
The Dread Mr. Darcy
The Scandalous Mr. Darcy
The Unraveling of Mr. Darcy

And fall in love with Mr. Darcy all over again